FEAR IS A MONSTER

MYRMAIDEN

A STORY OF MIDGATE

R. M. KROGMAN

Copyright © 2023 by R. M. Krogman

Cover art by Miblart | miblart.com
Artwork commissioned by the author.

Edited by Dylan Garity | garityediting.com

MYRMAIDEN

To the ones who don't fit in.

May you never endure the banality of an ordinary
existence.

Acknowledgments

Many thanks to my beta readers including G. Barrow, J. DeBoer, and T. Plyler for their time and comments, and especially C. Krogman, J. Krogman, and K. Krogman, who saw the roughest drafts of this story. Despite its raw form, you saw potential and told me to keep going. Your enthusiasm and critical feedback were both essential to making this the best story it can be.

A Note to Readers

Myrmaiden tells the backstory of a main character that you'll see again in the epic fantasy *The Keepers of Midgate*. This story is best read *between* the first and second books of the trilogy (*Liberation* and *Sundering*), although it can be read as a stand-alone. I strongly encourage you to read *Liberation* first.

If you like what you read and haven't already signed up for my newsletter, please remember to sign up at:

https://rmkrogman.com/join/

1

"Do you see it, Yuki?"

Her brother's eagerness broke through her daydream as Yuki gazed at the dance of rainbow light on the cavern floor. Refracted light beams shimmered across her skin, and she giggled with delight. She wriggled her bare toes in the soft sand of the floor in front of the water gate and marveled at the hues of violet and pink and yellow cascading across her legs.

"It's a whale. A sawtoothed whale, I think. Come look!" Tai grasped Yuki's slight shoulders and turned her, so that she faced the portal squarely.

Dragging her eyes from the riot of colors, Yuki searched the open sea beyond the gate, as Tai asked her to do.

Far off, a blue silhouette drifted eastward with languid pumps of its tail. Its shape was blurry with both distance and the slightly turbid murkiness of the ocean, but Tai was right. He was always right. The shape was a large sawtoothed whale, and the rest of the pod was beyond, revealed only as dim gray outlines. Yuki squinted.

Tai pulled her to the portal's edge, his eyebrows raised high with enthusiasm. "Let's go. Maybe it's the one we saw last year." He moved through the water gate—a massive vertical wall of water with a magically smooth surface. As he stepped out, his leading foot quickly morphed, flattening and spreading into a half flipper. The second foot followed, and his bare, copper-skinned legs melded effortlessly. His human hand still gripped hers, though, and he gently tugged her through the gate with an encouraging, toothy smile. He was so good at shifting, so good at keeping his balance midstep as he moved from air to water and back. In that moment between worlds, Yuki often lost her balance.

She concentrated on shifting. First, to breathe. Her nose shuttered, and gills rippled open along her neck. She took a deep inhale, undulating the sea's cool, refreshing water through her throat and into her altered lungs. Bubbles escaped her grinning mouth as water replaced the last of the air.

That was the best part of shifting to myrform. The water flooding her airways tasted salty, followed by an aftertaste of sweet coral and kelp. Its sweetness lingered on the back of her tongue.

Next, her bone structure adjusted. This part was a little less comfortable, especially the stretching of her spine and the shortening of her leg bones. The higher form required a lot of tissue alteration, but Yuki had been learning how to shift since she was a toddler. Like all myr, she could do it—it was an inborn ability, what set them apart from the common humans who polluted the earth above. She watched her scrawny legs, bare-skinned beneath her skirted breechbelt, become one. Everything below her belly button shifted and compressed, forming a perfect tail with flutters of yellow fin.

She chirped happily at Tai, who merely smiled back. He floated at ease, maintaining a steady position with subtle flickers of his yellow fins, edged with white. His hand clutched hers, helping her orient as she gained her bearings.

"Come on," he clicked, switching to the underwater language of the myr.

Still holding hands, they swam together toward the distant creature.

The gray-blue shape coalesced into a clearer silhouette, and Tai called out with a low groan crossing the span between them. The sound shivered through the water, and the creature responded. Making a lazy circle, it headed toward them. Yuki squealed with excitement, her grip tightening on Tai's hand, and they hastened to meet it.

As the whale approached, Yuki chirped again with pleasure and surprise. It *was* the same whale. She bore a unique combination of mottling on her nose and sides, a vermiculation of browns and tans and whites that marked her. She was a matron, but the calf from last year was no longer at her side. It had likely joined the main pod and was somewhere nearby, moving northward along the migratory route that passed by Shiggo City.

Then, a small shape detached from the big whale, skirting around her side to hide behind her tail.

Yuki grabbed Tai's sleeve and pointed. "She had another baby!"

Tai grinned and shushed her gently. "Shy little one, isn't he?"

The calf hid, but Yuki could see the bright splotches of color. Some echoed the patterns on his mother, but his whites seemed whiter and his darks seemed darker. Only babies had such defined colors, such sharp lines and edges. Tai said it was to help them blend into the kelp shadows when they were most vulnerable.

The cow circled them, happily clicking a social greeting and darting up and down in the water column. She groaned; she was pleased to see them as well, and more than a little curious at their strangeness.

Yuki giggled. Wild sawtooths were always curious, as eager to examine humans as humans were to examine them. It was no wonder the myr had domesticated them. Still, Yuki wasn't the strange one. She was myr, through and through, the proud offspring of the greatest lineage of myr warriors in history, Queen Noriko and King Kenji. That was what Tai said, in any case.

They both clicked reassurances to the dowager whale, jointly projecting friendliness and safety in the shared language of emotions and simple vocabulary. The calf peeked out from behind his mother, cautiously attentive to their conversation.

Satisfied, the large creature circled one last time before calling them to join her as she continued east and north. Her path was predestined and well-known, taking her through the straits toward Fumaya, and then on to the cool waters of the Merchan Sea. She would lead them safely through, just as she led the rest of her pod.

Yuki followed the whale's trajectory and spied the distant shapes of the other whales, still far out to sea in a large group. They responded to her call with throaty groans that echoed through the water in a musical cacophony. They were coming.

The great dowager slid farther away from the two children, her calf conjoined to her side, and became first a blurry shape before melting into the deep blue beyond.

Tai and Yuki swam slowly back to the coastal shelf together, both lost in their own peaceful daydreams.

How far she must have come with her little one. How far did she still have to go? What was it like in the cold Merchan Sea? Were there kelp forests like in Shiggo, or did the plants change, host to a forest of strange creatures she had never seen? Or were there steep rocky cliffs dropping to the bottom of the sea, like in the Lai'akala Trench? That place had always scared Yuki a little bit. Did the whale have other myr friends who visited her, not Shiggon-jin but perhaps Fumayan-jin or Merchan-jin?

They arrived at the gate, and again Tai led the way, gaining the ground before turning to help Yuki. She leaned into him as she focused on each process of shifting: lungs, head, bones.

She squirmed her reformed toes in the soft white sand once again. It was almost as wonderful as being in the ocean in myrform, but not quite.

To be accepted by the sawtoothed whale, to be one with the water and the fish and the animals. To belong. Nothing was better than that feeling.

She hugged Tai, and he faked a wheezing breath.

"You're so strong," he chuckled. Then he squeezed her back, wrapping his long arms around her and lifting her off the floor. She shrieked as he spun her around, and she heard the gate guards' light laughter in the background. Her brother grinned as he returned her to the ground, breathless. "She remembered us. You could tell by the tone she used; it's what they use for pod members. She was happy to see us again."

Yuki caught her breath and then frowned. "Her other calf was missing."

The lopsided curl of Tai's lips froze, and he leaned down to look at her more closely. "Don't worry,

Yuki-sho. She was just ahead of the rest of the pod, and I'm sure her calf from last year is okay."

"How do you know? How do you know it didn't get lost or hurt?"

He sighed through his nose. "You always think of things like that, but she's a good mother. Remember, this is her fourth calf."

"But why wasn't the third one *with* her?"

"He was old enough," Tai said. "Don't be sad. It's a good thing for life to move forward. He can't be a baby forever, and if he was, she wouldn't be able to have another one yet."

Yuki stared out the Whale Gate, aptly named for its vista facing the migration current. She chewed on his words. Tai *was* always right, but how did he really know? The distant shapes of the whale pod were gone. The great blue of the Mana Loi seemed to go on forever, a vast world of unknown adventure and beauty.

"Do you think she has other friends?"

Tai's smile returned. "You mean like us? Sure. Anyone can see she's friendly. I'll bet she meets some Fumayan-jin on her way through the strait."

Yuki's eyes widened. "Do you think they go all the way to the ice? Won't they be cold?"

Her brother laughed. "It's not always covered in ice, especially in the summertime. They'll go to the thick sweetgrass beds and enjoy the abundance of sparfish, and her baby will grow, and then they'll come back. Next time we see her, her calf won't be as timid, and they'll linger more on the return."

Yuki pondered that. Although she was a little irked not to have seen the rest of the pod up close, she knew they'd be by again. She had always liked sawtooths, but they were fearsome and could be difficult to break and ride. The master marshal had instructed her to take a blackheaded whale first, a slightly smaller and more biddable animal. All she knew was that she loved the predatory sawtooths. They were so beautiful, so graceful, one with the ocean and with each other. They moved in such synchrony—that was the word Tai used—and seemed so tightly knit with each other. She didn't imagine them bickering like she and Kei did, and she didn't imagine the dowager ever disciplining her calves with a mean spirit. However, she did imagine them hunting together, playing off each other as they corralled a hapless group of sparfish. Tai had even said they killed lone sharks, just like myr did.

She huffed and screwed up her face, pouting her lower lip out. She didn't want to wait for them to come back.

Tai mussed her hair and teased her for being dramatic. "Be patient. They'll return after a season north, just like they always do."

"You messed up my braids," Yuki scowled as fiercely as she could at him and tried to fix her hair but then collapsed against him, giggling. He was right. Tai was always right.

She returned to the rainbow colors that shimmered across the sandy floor, hopping on one color at a time while dragging Tai by the hand. They moved away from the gate together, with Yuki balancing foot by foot and Tai stepping with her, a bemused smile upon his face.

2

Spring had arrived.

Yuki loved spring. The stormy swells of the wintry Mana Loi would calm, and the kelp forests beyond the edge of the farms would enliven with dense, lush foliage. The striated kelpfish and pincered shrimp, awakening from their torpor, would create a constant flutter of movement in the forest depths. Renewed light would shine down to the sea bottom along the outskirts of Shiggo City, and the sea farms would be planted. Above, on the land, the dry soil would be tilled and seeded as well, and the trade ships would arrive in droves.

The city always got busy afterward, especially on the surface. Most high-ranking visitors stayed at Shiggo Castle, the magnificent multileveled seat of House ol'Kada ol'Tatami, filling the elaborate guest suites on the second and third lower levels. If they were human, they stayed in the upper levels, which weren't as nice, but then, they didn't have that many human visitors. Nurse said the lower levels made humans uncomfortable, but Yuki didn't understand the reason for that. The lower levels were where the Lower Market was, and the Water Temple, and the bulk of the castle including her and Kei's bedroom, and everything else important.

She sang to herself, playing alone as she often did. Not really alone—she had Chala. Her doll's long black hair, spun and braided from coarse ink-dyed horsehair, was much like Yuki's own. Yuki had tied beads into Chala's hair so they clacked and rattled against each other whenever the doll swayed in her hands. It was musical and rhythmic, a clatter of emphasis to accompany Chala's imaginary conversation. The doll kept her company so she wouldn't be alone, because myr should never be by themselves.

"Suppertime, Yuki-sho." A cheerful voice echoed through the cave in which Yuki sat. A matronly woman approached and scooped her into her soft, age-wrinkled arms for a hug. "Come along now. Your father has guests; we must get you ready."

"Can I keep Chala with me?" Yuki clutched the doll to her heart.

"Yes, dearie."

"Good." Satisfied she wouldn't be forced into a room of strangers without her comforting companion, she allowed Nurse to guide her through the main castle passageway and up a broad staircase. Then they turned down a side passage to the children's quarters along the outer wall.

Her sister, Keiki, was already dressed and sitting somewhat sullenly on the bed, trying to keep her frock from getting too wrinkled. Pearl strings and chains of tiny seashells drew back her hair. She gave Yuki a look.

"You're late," she mouthed, then subtly glanced toward the chair where Mother sat, bouncing their baby brother, Tan.

Mother immediately stood and delegated Tan to Kei, who took him stiffly. "Mama, what if he makes a mess?" she whined.

Mother ignored her, instead sizing up Yuki and pursing her lips. "Where have you been?" she chided, shaking her head. "We *must* get you changed for suppertime, quickly. An important delegation arrived."

"I'm already dressed, Mama!"

Mother shook her head again, exasperated, and strode to the chest along the wall. She waved at Nurse to oblige her, and the old woman gently removed Yuki's thin leather shirt, working the casual outfit around her arms so that she didn't have to relinquish Chala. The breechcloth skirt's colored beads clinked like Chala's hair as it dropped to the floor, and Mother slipped a longer, more formal shift over her head, one which draped all the way to her knees. Its sleeves reached her elbows. Over that, Mother pulled down a shimmery, scaled leather smock that shone in iridescent shades of blue and green. The top was ribbed and stretchy, while the bottom flowed loose around her hips. Silver gilded the edges in scalloped patterns.

Finally, Mother hung a ceremonial breechbelt around Yuki's waist, instead of her usual one. Its construction was silver-alisite, shining beautifully but resistant to rust or tarnish. Instead of fringes of leather or beads, the belt hung with chains of tiny gemstones, twisted and braided together with silver thread. The central adornment, which covered the front of her pelvis, was a great abalone shell, worked and carefully honed into a rectangular shape and edged in more gemstones.

It matched Kei's. The perfect design of the nacreous shell implied her high status, but like all breech-belts, symbolic rankstones also indicated her position as a princess of Shiggo.

Mother quickly reined her lengths of hair back with pearl strings, again just like Kei's. She turned Yuki's slight shoulders toward her and looked her up and down with a small, satisfied smile.

"There. Now perhaps you'll be acceptable to receive our guests. Behave yourselves at table, both of you." Mother eyed both girls with a severe sternness.

This meeting must be important, Yuki thought. She didn't care much for all the serious talk that happened at court; it usually had to do with trade routes and prices and currents. As thirdborn, she didn't need to worry too much about it either, and she didn't. After all, there were far more interesting things to do, like playing with Chala or watching Kei train at the garrison or exploring the gardens with Tai. She smiled up at Mother.

"I'll be good, Mama," she promised. "You look so pretty."

Mother rose and stood tall. She really was beautiful. Maybe she was the most beautiful person in the world, just like Father was the most handsome and Tai was the smartest.

Yuki realized that Mother was formally dressed as well, her elegant gown trailing behind her with an asymmetrical cut, as was traditional. Most of her dress was gold and yellow, with an incredible shimmering cape hanging from the central rondel behind her shoulders. Its edges affixed to each elbow, making it flare outward. Even the scallop shells of her jewelry were species with a beige cast to their white shells, and her gems were topaz and tourmaline. Her breechbelt was gold, and its fringes were pure jasper, with each bead carved into the shape of a fish. That was the one she wore for the most official occasions, where she had to be the Queen of Shiggo and not just Yuki's mother.

That meant Yuki had to be extra well-behaved.

Mother briefly smiled, then looked from one girl to the other. "My daughters," she murmured. "Make me proud." She waved a hand at Kei—who returned little Tan to her waiting arms—then swept out of the room, leading the way to the dining hall.

Kei huffed quietly, scanning her outfit for spittle. Then she smoothed her dress with care and stood.

Yuki danced over to her, one hand on Chala and one reaching for her sister. "Let's eat, Kei-sho. I'm starving!"

Like Mother, Kei allowed a small, pert smile, slightly affectionate but closely controlled so as not to ruin the ochre on her lips. She carried so much more dignity than Yuki did. Maybe *she* would be the most beautiful person in the world when she was older, instead of Mother. She looked so refined for her age—she wasn't all that much older than Yuki, just a few years.

Kei took her hand, and they proceeded out with Nurse trailing behind.

Tai joined them in the hallway, emerging from his room fully dressed in similarly formal attire. He complimented them both, and Kei beamed. After a brisk ascent to the surface level, up the wide staircase with its glass roof to let the sun shine in, they stepped into the west hall.

Upon their arrival, Steward Welian's voice rang out announcing the queen's entrance. Mother glided to the high tables, her dress shimmering like the Eye above, and sat between Father and a nobly dressed woman with a haughty demeanor. They greeted each other with polite nods.

To Father's right sat a nobly dressed man with a very square face and a prominent forehead, pale skin with a dull cast similar to the conch shells she collected in the garden, and a light smattering of freckles on his ruddy arms. His nose was rather large. All of his features seemed large, in fact, sticking out of his face farther than they should.

Yuki stifled a giggle.

Both foreign nobles wore heavy-looking golden crowns with dyed fur trimmings, and Yuki recognized them as the royals of Krita. Humans. Their strange clothes bore the bright blue hue of House Crayer, trimmed with delicate lace collars, trailing lace-trimmed sleeves, poofy doublets and bustles, and dangling pearls. Yuki wanted to laugh at their funny outfits but strangled it in her throat after a glance at Mother. *Make me proud, my daughters.*

Tai led them to their own spots, intermingled with other children who also wore Crayer blue. Yuki clutched Kei's hand and sighed a small squeak of relief as she got a place next to her sister. Tai, meanwhile, sat two spots away. A boy about Kei's age sat between Kei and Tai. Yuki found herself sitting next to a second boy on her left, and she forced a civil greeting.

This boy was younger, with a shy demeanor and a tentative smile. His cheeks bore as many freckles as his father's, and his sandy hair hung like a dirty mop on his head.

Yuki gasped as Kei ripped her hand away beneath the table and turned her shoulders slightly away. What was she looking at, and why was she smiling so sweetly? Yuki didn't understand and tried to hold her sister's hand once again. This time, Kei turned and berated her in a few sharp but quiet words, then turned back to the older boy with full attention.

That one had much shorter hair and fewer freckles than the boy next to her, but still that odd color.

Although Yuki pouted, Kei chattered on, oblivious. With a sigh, Yuki tightened her hold of Chala. She hated when Kei acted like this. It usually happened around the pages she said were "cute," but this seemed worse. Pages didn't eat meals at their table, distract them with unwanted conversation, or sit between them. She leaned forward to catch her brother's eye, but he was even farther away and equally distracted.

Master Merridan, the resident Waterpriest assigned to the royal castle, stood and droned a mealtime prayer, raising his arms high over the group with powerful authority. Yuki didn't listen to the words, although she did like Master Merridan. It was the same prayer the Waterpriests always spoke over supper, and she knew the intonation by heart. Finally he sat, and servants emerged from the buttery and kitchens with bowls and platters.

Black crab stew appeared in front of her, and the savory scent made her nostrils flare. A clatter of silverware arose, along with muted conversation from the high table. Mother and Father seemed open and friendly with their guests, even the somewhat stiff-looking Crayer woman.

Yuki puzzled her way through that. Mother had said that an important delegation had arrived, but these people were only humans. Shiggo didn't treat with the land kingdoms often, and Tai said there was a reason for that. Humans weren't trustworthy. They didn't follow the Way of the Current, they worshiped a false god, and they thought they were better than the myr. Why would Father invite them here?

"What is it?" A plaintive whisper reached her. The little boy next to her poked at the stew with his spoon, a worried expression on his face.

Yuki looked in his bowl. It was the same as hers. "Um, stew?" she replied with a shrug.

"But, what's it made of?" His thin eyebrows rose high in question, and his greenish eyes widened.

"Oh! Crab." She ladled a full spoon into her mouth as if to prove the soup was fine, then stopped short. Mother's scrutiny pierced the back of her head. She straightened in her chair and took smaller, daintier sips, being careful to dab at her mouth with a napkin between efforts. Table decorum was important, especially in front of guests.

The boy watched her eat doubtfully at first, then copied her with a tiny swallow of the broth. His big eyes widened even further. "It's good." He shoveled more down without any semblance of manners. Then he smacked his lips and smiled. "I'm Branig."

"Taiuki," she answered, frowning. "Have you never had crab before?"

Branig shook his head. "I have, but it never looked like this. I really like it though. Did you know we're visiting for a whole week? Father says we have to do . . . umm . . . *nagoshins*." He trailed off, squinting at the table and wrinkling one side of his nose.

"Negotiations." The older boy's voice cut in. He and Kei were both looking at them. "Your hair is pretty, like your sister's."

Kei grimaced, curling her ochred lips back with a carefully controlled expression. "Mama insists on dressing her like me. But she's just a silly little girl, still carrying her doll around everywhere." She turned her back on Yuki once again and continued chattering.

Yuki tightened her grip on Chala, who sat in her lap, and sullenly ate her stew. If only she could sit next to Tai, but he was all the way on the far side of the older boy, participating in their conversation with his usual animation. They were laughing, joking.

She sighed at the tedium of Branig's endless questions, answering only as necessary. She couldn't stop herself from squirming in her seat. She wanted to go back to playing, resuming her game from prior to the meal, but Mother would never allow it with such distinguished guests.

The meal proceeded, interspersed with pleasant songs of the wind and sea from Songmaster Haupan. Trays of brine-cooked shrimp, sauteed scallops with a zesty orange sauce, whole fish scaled and rubbed with seasonings and baked in butter, and roasted red meats. Next, a large platter with three shore-birds surrounded by soft-boiled speckled eggs. Yuki brightened. She explained to Branig how rare the eggs were, how perfectly the chefs cooked them to achieve the best flavor, and she helped him sprinkle the right salt on top from the selection at their table. He seemed confused at having to take servings from the shared platters on his own, and she caught herself giggling despite her discomfort at the strangeness of the visitors. Branig was so odd. Then pies appeared stuffed with meats, fish, and fruit.

When dessert finally came and went, the children were excused from the hall but told to stay together. Yuki relinquished hope of returning to her play. Maybe tomorrow would be better.

3

L ED BY T AI, THEY moved eagerly along past rooms and guards, out the castle entrance to the public mainway. Several Kritali guards followed at a quiet distance, apparently escorting them. Yuki asked about their overbearing presence, but Kei rolled her eyes and told her not to worry about it.

They wandered down a level, descending the wide main staircase. Godrig, the older boy, kept stride with Tai, emulating his proud bearing and taking the steps two at a time like he did. Kei hurried after them, abandoning Yuki altogether. Godrig made conversation about his own castle, the big ship they had sailed on from Krita, and how strange Shiggo City's layout was. None of it struck Yuki as complimentary, more like he was trying to impress them with how much better Krita was. He even commented on the scent of the air as they descended, but all Yuki could smell was the richness of sea air, the fullness of an environment bursting with life.

Branig nearly stumbled on the steps as he stared up at the ceiling. The entire mainway was open to the sky, protected by both a barrier of clear glass and the powerful magika of the Waterpriests, which kept the entirety of the lower castle levels dry. Branig's jaw hung slack as he realized he could see the clouds above. "We don't have anything like this at home," he marveled in a soft voice.

Yuki caught him as he tripped, and he gave her a sheepish but admiring look. "Will you hold my hand?" he asked hopefully, extending his palm out in supplication.

She acquiesced, clutching Chala in her other arm. Branig's smaller fingers were pale but warm, and he clung to her hand the way she would have done with Kei. Secure in her grip, he returned to looking at the ceiling, then cast his inspection around the entirety of the public mainway with a faint smile. The mainway was a long, slowly descending hall that connected Shiggo City's upper and lower levels. It was late enough to be fairly quiet, but a few myr citizens walked their waterdogs or went about their own hurried business.

All moved aside for the royal entourage with respectful salutes and bows.

When they reached the first portal, Godrig and Branig halted and stared.

Situated at the end of a long, cavernous side hall, the Whale Gate glistened in the low light of evening. A single guard lounged to one side, at ease given the sparse traffic. He straightened upon noticing them from afar.

Yuki noticed Branig's wonder and grinned. This was her favorite place, the best portal for whale-watching due to its direction facing the open migratory pathways over the farm fields. The entire Mana Loi was beyond, the glorious open sea.

"What is that?" Godrig asked. His awe seemed more doubtful than Branig's, his heavier brow scrunched tightly into a distrustful wrinkle in the middle. His glossy blue eyes matched the ocean waves, with a hint of green like Branig's.

Tai raised a single eyebrow. That always made Yuki laugh—he had been practicing it for a while.

"The Whale Gate," he answered, crossing his arms.

"That's a . . . gate? Like a city gate?" Godrig continued staring for a while, then scoffed. "Let's go look."

The children wandered toward the massive vertical wall of water, one of many carefully controlled interfaces between the air-filled mainway and the underwater portions of Shiggo City. The sounds of the ocean echoed in, amplified by the cave walls. The water beyond was dim; the sun had set minutes before.

Godrig swaggered over to the portal, then tentatively reached out and brushed the water with his fingertips. Ripples exuded outward but dissipated quickly, forced back to a perfectly flat, clear surface by the Waterpriests' magika. Then Godrig stuck his hand fully through, glancing back at Kei with a confident air. "Not so scary," he said.

For some reason, Kei mooned at him. "Most people that aren't from here are afraid of the water gates," she gushed.

"What's to fear?" Tai's derision rang out clearly, echoing through the hollow room. He stood tall, shoulders straight. He was taller than anyone else, being the oldest, and his stature made him look like

Father. "It's a gate, with more of Shiggo City on the other side."

Godrig's cheeks reddened, and the other children quieted as tension mounted between the two boys. Then he seemed to recover with a sneer. "It doesn't look like much of a city. I don't see proper streets or houses. Looks pretty uncivilized to me."

Tai frowned. "This is the Whale Gate. It faces more eastward. If you want to see more of the city, we should go to the Lower Market or the Garrison Gate."

Godrig jutted his chin out and seemed to shake his head a little. "I doubt they're that impressive, being locked into these mucky cave walls. *Our* city has a bunch of markets, not just one, and our garrison is massive, with multiple barracks and an entire fleet of ships."

Yuki had never before seen the look that came over her brother's face in that moment, but it made her heart darken toward Godrig. The boy was rude. He might be older like Tai, but he obviously didn't know anything about anything. She thrust Chala at him like a weapon. "No one has a bigger army than Shiggo. Our military is the best in the world! But you'll never see it because you're afraid to go to the Garrison Gate."

Godrig turned his glower from Tai to her. "Shut up. You're just a stupid little girl."

Tai shoved him in the shoulder and stepped in front of Yuki. "Don't talk to my sister that way," he growled.

The two older boys glared at each other, the suffocating silence broken only by the clicks and taps and bubbling pops echoing from the gate.

Next to Yuki, Branig tentatively touched the gate interface, his eyes wide. "*I* wouldn't want to go through. It's dark out there."

That seemed to distract Godrig, or maybe it gave him a safe excuse to break away from Tai's intense scrutiny. "You can barely swim anyway, Branig," Godrig said with a snort of false laughter. "Why would you go swim in that miserable darkness anyway?"

"That's our city," Tai snarled, raising his voice again.

"*I* can swim," Kei interrupted, her voice sweet and wheedling. "I'm a great swimmer, so you'd be safe with me, Prince Branig. And, I have a beautiful tail." She tossed her hair, making the pearls and shells clack together.

Godrig tried to pull a suave look at Kei, although his cheeks were still flushed from embarrassment, and the wrinkle in his brow didn't actually go away. Was that what Tai meant when he said smiles didn't always reach people's eyes?

Kei continued. "Our Waterpriest taught me how to shift to myrform when I was only two summers old."

"All of us learned when we were two summers old, Kei." Tai's impatience was obvious. "And no one needs to see your tail. It's not their way, on land. They won't understand."

Godrig was indignant. "I'm not afraid of any water gate or the dark, and I know what a myrperson is. I'm not stupid."

"Fooled me," Tai replied sharply.

Branig and Yuki swung back and forth between the two as they began shouting. Tai never shouted. Kei first tried to shush him, then started to shout too, demanding Tai stop embarrassing her.

Yuki scowled at the scene, feeling the world whirling around them in a blur. She didn't understand exactly what they were fighting about, but she knew she didn't like Godrig, and she knew Tai was right. These people couldn't understand myr ways;

they were only human. Why did they even show their Kritali guests the Whale Gate in the first place when they couldn't appreciate it? This fighting was exactly why myr kept to themselves, why they schooled together. It made them stronger against their enemies, which included people from the land kingdoms.

"Children!" Nurse appeared and forcibly separated the two boys. She glared at Tai especially, then Kei and Yuki. "Children, your mother would be ashamed. These boys are guests of Shiggo, and you must treat them as such." She studied each of them. Yuki picked at Chala's braids; Nurse's stern looks were best avoided. But Nurse tipped her chin up and met her eye, a direct challenge for dominance. "Do you understand, dearies?"

Yuki couldn't keep the tears from welling up, and she met Nurse's regard with wet cheeks and sniffles. She nodded and looked back down. The woman relented somewhat, affectionately placing her hand on Yuki's head, then looked at Tai.

He and Kei were staring at the sandy floor as well. Tai touched his forehead in a sign of respect. "We shall conform, Nurse," he mumbled. Kei made a noncommittal sound but echoed his salute. Nurse was in charge.

Seemingly satisfied, she backed away. "Behave. I'll be back later to fetch the boys to their room for the night." She turned and left, passing the two Kritali soldiers who lingered as far from the Whale Gate as possible while still overseeing their young charges. Nurse's footsteps echoed back all the way until she turned the corner to the mainway.

The portal loomed.

Tai and Godrig returned to glaring at each other. Tai looked so much like Father in that moment, regal in his aquamarine cape and silver rondels and silver-gold twisted breechbelt.

Godrig was nothing like him beyond stubborn assertiveness. His watery eyes and sickly pallor contrasted with Tai's rich bronze skin and black gaze. His shoulders, though starting to widen with a bulkier set, were still a finger lower than Tai's, and he had to look slightly up with his jutting chin. The edges of his thin lips curled up in a nasty expression.

"If you're such a good swimmer, why don't you prove it, myr boy?" Godrig's voice was cold. "Don't look to your wetnurse. Or are you going to 'conform' like an obedient dog?"

Yuki dropped Branig's hand and shoved the older boy in the stomach. "He can prove it anytime!" she cried. "He's the best and strongest swimmer in the whole ocean."

Godrig shoved her with one hand, and she toppled backward, landing heavily on her rear. "Don't touch me, brat, and don't talk back."

Yuki could see Tai take a deep breath and tense, but before he could do anything, she scrambled to her feet and shoved herself in Godrig's face once more. "I'm not even the strongest *or* the biggest, but I'm still stronger and better than you!" she screamed.

With that, she dove through the gate and shifted, glaring at Godrig as her legs melded together. He failed to cover his astonishment as her fin emerged beneath her breechbelt and short skirt.

Tai flashed a winning smile at her and, with slightly more dignity, threw off his cape. "Watch this," he declared as he stepped through the portal. He transformed effortlessly, his legs conjoining to form a lithe gray tail with white edges on the frills. He turned to Yuki and switched to clicking, declaring he would handle putting Godrig in his place. "Proud of you, Yuki-sho." He winked, then whipped his powerful tail and shot upward and away.

The other children pushed their noses to the portal's edge, peering through the darkening sea to watch. Tai became a dim figure as he reached the distant surface, and then they saw a splash as he executed a high flip in the air.

An impressed shout echoed through the gate, and Yuki spared a glance at the Kritali visitors. Branig was thrilled, grabbing Kei's hand in his excitement. Kei was trying to shake him off, her lips tight at the unwelcome touch. Godrig was at first speechless, then seemed to recover. He sneered at Yuki.

"I guess you can swim, but so can I. And *without* a tail or some kind of polluted magic." He crossed his arms more tightly, acting nonchalant, but his gaze kept flitting toward the surface and her talented brother.

Yuki glowered as she had seen Tai do, then turned away to watch his return. From the open sea, he began swimming back to the Whale Gate almost leisurely, a cocksure grin on his face.

A behemoth shadow materialized from the dark ocean and smashed into him from the side. His shrill cry reverberated through the water, and time slowed. Yuki saw everything between heartbeats. The shark came from the darkness, a massive beast. Nearly black on top, a shocking white on its belly. Hundreds of razored teeth stacked in rows, and its gape seemed the size of her entire body. Hooking scars marred its side, and one of its pectoral fins was damaged and misshapen. Beady, death-hungry eyes glared, its attention fully set upon its naive prey.

Those terrible jaws clamped solidly around Tai's midsection, and then it whipped from side-to-side until Yuki heard the awful sound of tissue tearing and bones snapping.

She screamed as the faint taste of blood hit her gills.

Without hesitation, she thrust her tail as hard as she could, pumping toward Tai. She had to get to him. She had to save him. He was still alive.

The shark whipped him again, and a chunk tore off. Tai's innards drifted out, a tangled mass of smooth intestines and bloody carnage, and a raw organ flavor hit Yuki's tongue. Tai wasn't struggling anymore. His expression was oddly blank, and the sunshine-yellow flecks of his eyes had dulled somehow, like clouds blocking a starry sky. The shark took another piece off, mad with the thrill and flavor of violence.

Yuki realized as she struggled toward him that she wasn't getting any closer. She glimpsed back at the unexpected pinch on her tail. Kei clutched her fin, her grip so tight her fingers had turned white beneath their painted nails. She pulled as hard as she could, fighting Yuki's forward motion. Yuki shrieked at her as she felt herself losing the fight. Why did she have to be smaller? She tumbled through the portal, ungainly, her hands still reaching toward Tai. She fell into a pile on top of Kei, who panted with the effort.

Then her sister wailed, all of her rouge and make-up coursing in rivulets down her cheeks.

Godrig stood by dumbly, his formerly set jaw hanging slack as he stared, and Branig screamed. The gate guard staggered to a knee, his own failure overwhelming. He stumbled away, shouting an alarm down the hall. The Kritali guards were likewise frozen in horror, and he pushed past them with a sob.

Yuki wasn't aware of her shifting legs, the reemergence of her toes or splitting of her limbs, the shuttering of her gills, which had tasted everything. She wasn't aware of Kei shoving her aside and yelling at her. She was only aware of the wretched world beyond the gate. She couldn't look away from Tai.

Only his head remained.

The monster investigated the bony remnant. Then, losing interest, it slid silently into the darkness.

Spinning and tumbling slowly with empty orbs—those eyes once so full of cleverness and humor and life—Taifun's head sank away from sight.

4

The myr are one with the Water, and the Water is one with the myr. The myr can attain a godly form by embracing the Water and shedding the weaker elements. A oneness with the Water is a oneness with the Most High.

The Way of the Current

YUKI SAT CROSS-LEGGED IN front of the Kelp Gate, staring out. She picked absent-mindedly at the clacking beads of Chala's hair; they rattled a distant song of childhood that seemed less familiar than it had once been. She ignored the dimmed rainbow hues cast upon the floor from the angle of the portal as it caught the sun perfectly.

It was quieter here. The deeper she went, the quieter it got.

After the initial spring transplanting of sporophytes, the farmers reduced their use of the Kelp Gate, and no one else really needed it until harvest season. There weren't even guards posted here at the portal interface, just farther in where the gate foyer met the mainway. Swaying in the ocean on the other side of the portal, thick patches of cultured greenery extended from Shiggo City's edges outward for leagues.

Yuki examined the young kelp fields with dull eyes. There was little movement compared to some of the other city gates, little cover for fishes and only a few farmholds scattered between expansive fields. That would change as the kelp grew and thickened, forming orderly grids of color depending on species. The maroon ones with spindly foliage were red sugar kelp, one of her favorites. Tai would have known what all of them were.

She had moved to the Kelp Gate since it happened.

She couldn't bear to face the Whale Gate, the place with the best and worst memories now melded together in an inexorable combination. She couldn't recall the dowager whale without recalling the pucker of Taifun's guts. Couldn't recall the joy in his smile without the fear in his eyes or the beady hate in the shark's. Couldn't hear the throaty calls and groans of the passing pods without also hearing the terrible thump as the beast smashed into Tai's side, the rending of teeth upon flesh, the tearing and snapping.

How was her brother just *gone*? How could everything go so wrong and not be fixable? She had never faced something Tai couldn't fix, and she had never considered the possibility that some things were beyond redemption.

How could he leave her so alone?

Hot tears coursed down her cheeks, dripping off her chin onto Chala's head, and she muffled her cries by biting her lip. She wiped her eyes with a sleeve. "Why did you have to leave, Tai-sho?" she whispered.

Her voice barely bounced back from the portal face, sounding oddly hollow. Even her echo had left her alone.

A sudden black fury filled her, and she stood, facing the sea. She flung Chala at the gate and screamed. "Why did you have to leave?" The shrieking last syllables did bounce back, amplified by the vertical wall of water and teasing her with their fading repetition. *Leave, leave, leave.*

Chala slumped as she hit the water, but the magika of the portals allowed her to pass through with hardly a ripple, and she caught in the light current that moved past the Kelp Gate. She drifted away in a ponderous tumble, beaded braids and head over shoeless heels, and again Tai's final moments flashed through Yuki's mind.

She gasped, horrified, and reached ineffectually for the doll. It was just beyond her grasp.

Even though it was daytime, she hesitated. But no, Chala was spinning away and would soon be lost. She dove forward through the gate in a panic, shifting as she went, her focus entirely on her precious retreating toy.

But no air came.

Her nostrils burned with saltwater, and her scrawny bare legs flailed. She couldn't see anything through her blurred vision, and her eyes felt like fire. She cried out, and bubbles erupted from her mouth. She sucked in water when she gasped.

Yuki felt the hard beads and soft body of Chala hit her searching hand, and she grasped the doll frantically. Where was the gate? She thrashed about, thinking maybe she saw it to the left in the haze. Her swimming was wild and without coordination. She couldn't remember the last time she had tried to swim with legs, swim by kicking. The gentle swish of the kelp fields escalated to a roar, and the world spun. She couldn't orient up or down, left or right, and she wasn't sure whether it was the ocean or her own body that turned. Her vision kept clouding, then slamming inward and pulsing out. Everything darkened around her, as though the Eye far above on the surface was winking out.

She tumbled unexpectedly through the gate, slamming into the ground, barely conscious. The last thing she saw was Nurse, who was never very far. Yuki tried to blink enough to see clearly, but every-thing was hazy and burning. The woman began to go through the motions of magically expressing water from lungs as Yuki faded into a terrifying, suffocating darkness.

Murmuring roused her. Yuki lay prone, tucked tightly into her bed with a light fur laid over. A weight sat heavy upon her chest and crushed her into the soft mattress.

Both Mother and Father peered over her, their brows knotted with identical consternation and doubt. Father ground his jaw back and forth as Mother's lips moved. Yuki couldn't remember her mother ever looking so worried before.

Nurse was on her other side, busily arranging bowls on a food tray. The little platters and cup and silverware looked ready to serve, and yet she continually moved things around, setting the teacup just so and the spoon perfectly aligned with the fork.

"She didn't shift?" Father looked at Nurse, his dark eyebrows—*just like Tai's*—lifting in query.

Nurse's lips turned down at the corners, emphasizing the increasingly prominent smile wrinkle that had once been a dimple. She shook her head and rearranged something on the tray, as if keeping her hands busy might allow her not to face King Rentai directly. Father could be intimidating when he used that tone.

He stared at her for a few brief moments, then cast an eye at Mother, who pursed her lips tightly. They both seemed to shake their heads.

Waterpriest Merridan glided in with his apprentice mage on his heels. Both were quite somber, their faced molded and frozen in the expression they used in temple rituals: emotionless, steady, serious. Merridan always wore that face for official sermonizing, but Yuki liked when he smiled. As the Waterpriest assigned most frequently to the castle, Master Merridan knew her family better than most, led their prayers and praises, and helped them understand their inborn myr magic. Merridan edged Nurse out of the way and settled in a chair next to the bed. It creaked under his weight. He peered at Yuki, seeing she was awake. "Bright day and I'ya's blessings, my child. How are you feeling?" His formal tone didn't reflect the gentleness of his touch as he patted her hand.

"My chest hurts." And it did. It felt like someone was pressing their boot on her ribs, like she couldn't get enough air no matter how many breaths she took.

"Yes, my dear princess, you were . . ." He paused uncomfortably, then cleared his throat several times. "Drowning," he finished. The word sounded foreign on his tongue.

What? Myr didn't drown. Myr *couldn't* drown.

"Do you remember what happened, my child?"

Yuki thought hard. She had jumped through the portal to grab Chala, but for some reason everything had gone hazy. The water had hit her, embraced her, then tightened its hold to a terrifying and inescapable immersion. A great, icy fear had clenched her body then, as it did now. Paralysis locked her in place on the bed, even as she felt the world swaying madly, and she realized she was gripping Master Merridan's first two fingers in her own.

"The water . . ." she whispered. Her words felt phlegmy and thick, and she hacked a sickly cough.

Merridan patted her hand again. "Surely, you know the water is a part of you, as you are a part of it. There is nothing to fear in Water." His calm tone was meant to reassure, but for once it didn't diminish the queasiness in Yuki's stomach. "Do you understand, Yuki-sho? Nothing to fear—"

She sat up suddenly and vomited, as though her entire body rejected the idea of returning to the sea.

Tai. Where was Tai when she needed him?

Merridan leaned away from the mess that sprayed across the furs, but he didn't relinquish her hand, and she didn't let go either. He kept speaking, that steady and reasonable drone of praying Waterpriests. "It will be all right, my child. You must let Taifun join the current, and remember your lessons. You are one with the Water, as it is meant to be and must be. You must swim, for you are myr."

Yuki whipped her head—*like the shark shook him, back and forth, back and forth*—and refused. "I don't want to swim anymore."

Mother let out a strange choking sound, somewhere between a gasp and a cough, then began to sob into Father's shoulder. Stoic as ever, he wrapped his arm around her and marched her out, leaving Yuki alone with the men of the Water Temple and Nurse. She heard their steps fade away, and a strange sadness balled up inside. The weight on her chest seemed to get heavier.

The apprentice towered silently over her from the foot of the bed, staring into her and through her. Maybe he was a sensitive, one who could read magical gifts and identify sources of power—and weakness. He grimaced, a look that failed to wrinkle his younger face. Leaning forward, he solemnly pulled Yuki's fingers off Merridan's. "She's lost the form. Can you not see it, Master?"

Merridan shook his head slightly. "No. No, she couldn't." His face turned tragic, and he resisted being pulled away by his apprentice. "No," he repeated, shaking the younger man off. He leaned over Yuki, ignoring the mess of vomit as he peered into her face. "Yuki-sho, you must swim again. I can sense your gifting. You will be as great as Taifun someday, greater even. The blood runs strong in you, the blood of House ol'Kada ol'Tatami. Do not fear the Water."

His intensity was frightening. His aggrieved face was too close, the only clear thing in a miserable blur. She could see the deepening of wrinkles that hadn't been so obvious before, the wetness of his yellow-flecked eyes, the salt-and-pepper streaking of his hair and beard. She could smell his breath—a combination of bitter green tea, pan-fried shrimp, and stir-fried vegetables—combined with his cologne and soap. His robes exuded both oil and peppermint, evidence of his time in his two favorite places: the Water Temple and the Lower Market. His warm fingers enveloped hers, and she clung to that grounding sensation.

Nevertheless, even he finally pulled away, his face twisted with grief. "My child, my beloved pupil, please don't give up. You are the second daughter of the great myr king Rentai and Queen Furuhaki, of the most powerful kingdom in the sea. You are of Shiggo, a place that spans both salt and soil, connecting disparate peoples above and below the waves. And most importantly, you are now second in line. You are to be commander of our fierce and terrible fleets, broker of peace and war, just like your uncle Sashiro. Yuki-sho, you must accept this, and swim again."

She sobbed. Everything he said terrified her, especially that last part, because it meant one thing and one thing only. Tai was gone. He was really gone, forever. She shouldn't be Second any more than Kei should be First.

The apprentice mage succeeded in pulling Master Merridan away. "It's no use, Master. Feel how faded she has become. She's lost the connection. She's a—"

"Don't say it, son."

"A landwalker, Master."

Merridan's breath caught, and he released her hand suddenly. As his face retreated from hers, the entire world seemed to turn and spin and blur again.

5

She had never really understood that word.

Landwalker.

It was a bad word, one she wasn't supposed to use, although she had heard Tai say it before when he spoke of the strange-looking visitors they occasionally received from distant places like Krita. He always delivered it with a wince, a combination of disgust for what it meant and shame for using the term. Even though he was older, words like that were still not acceptable, and he had always warned her not to repeat it. Especially in front of Mother and Father.

She understood it to mean that something was inherently wrong with the other person, that they weren't equal to her. Myr were myr, and landwalkers were "everyone else."

Now she understood it completely. It meant broken. It meant the person's connection to the Water was severed, and what was a person without their connection to Water?

What was she?

Master Merridan kept coming back, day after day after day, appearing intermittently between the spans of time where she was mostly alone. Mother and Father didn't visit often, although sometimes Mother stood at the door and chewed on her lip.

Yuki didn't attempt to rise from her bed at first, and large blocks of time seemed to dissolve as she lay in a foggy stupor, waiting for the constriction in her chest to go away. She didn't know if it was day or night, nor did she care. Her bed was next to Kei's in their shared room, and sometimes her sister was there, and sometimes she wasn't. Maybe that was how to tell if it was day or night . . .

Then, when she decided she wanted to get up, she was pushed back down and told she wasn't well yet. She pouted at her bedroom confinement, but her initiative to get out of bed seemed to spur Master Merridan to renewed attempts to connect with her.

At first, he begged her to try to shift, his calm pleas wavering through one ear and out the other.

Then, seeing her staunch refusal, he shifted to a more structured tactic that reminded her of her earliest childhood lessons. He brought teaching scrolls, rolls of vellum covered in scratching Shiggon-jin symbols, sheets of prayers and incantations, all the things they used to teach the younger children. He read them aloud, switching frequently between holy verse and practical advice.

She rarely responded, either digging into her refusal to do anything that would put her back into the ocean where Taifun had died, or blanking out as she ruminated on her memories.

When her chest stopped aching and her cough disappeared, Master Merridan reluctantly acknowledged that her bed confinement was over, and that she could be allowed to wander the castle once again. Walking around might be good for her health, and perhaps even seeing the water gates again as she slowly overcame her fear.

Yuki didn't think through any of it in terms of what it meant. She just wanted to be free to wander, to explore and think and ponder her memories, and most of all to get away from Master Merridan's constant hounding.

She thought of Tai constantly. She wished those thoughts revolved around his toothy smile and firm grip on her shoulder, his happy chirps and groans as he called to the sawtoothed whales who passed by Shiggo City. But they didn't. They circled endlessly around his contorted face as it drifted out of sight, around the snuffed-out life and dimmed sparkle of his eyes. They careened around how much his death tasted like bile and acid adhering to her gills and the back of her throat. How much the crunch of his bones sounded like the maceration of her supper, the grinding of teeth breaking through exoskeleton echoing in her skull.

How could she swim again, knowing he was out there with his bones spread across leagues and drifting farther each day?

She missed the water, the sense of oneness with the world, and yet she couldn't bring herself to enter it, or even touch it. A part of herself was dying, drowning and suffocating in the Air: the part of her that was of the ocean. If it disappeared completely, she really would be a landwalker, like Godrig and Branig, and she knew that was bad.

The strength of her people, what made them special in the eyes of I'ya, was their bond to Water. They all shared the gift of shifting to myrform, the gift of living in both land and sea. Those who were born broken, although very rare, were "disappeared" according to Kei, so as not to dilute the blood with what she called "inferior qualities." All myr were thus the same, all part of a glorious school of chosen people.

The premise that had once made Yuki so proud now lent only a sense of dread. She was not one of them.

As though running from this frightening truth, she found new places to hide, always at the lower gates, where she would tuck herself behind a rock or a barrel or a pile of nets and stare wistfully out. The people of Shiggo seemed oblivious to her or to the danger the water posed to their livelihood. They stood near the gates, chatting and exchanging goods, as though there were nothing to fear. They passed in and out, ignoring the ominous presence of guards, with hardly a glance into the sea to ensure there were no more monsters. Most even lived out there, populating Shiggo City's underwater half.

Sometimes, Nurse knew her whereabouts, following her small footsteps like an unwelcome shadow, and other times Yuki would successfully evade her to disappear for hours at a time. Eventually, however, she would wander back, Chala in tow, and trudge into her bedroom for another dreary night. She didn't sleep well, harassed by nightmares that made her cry, and every morning heralded another round of battling Merridan's will, another round of failure and frustration.

Mother and Father rarely visited. Mother lavished attention on Kei and Tan but would depart when Yuki came in, leaving Nurse with terse instructions to brush her hair and ensure she bathed. It had been so long since Mother brushed her hair, or since Father had given her a tight embrace. Maybe Yuki's condition was contagious, like a disease. Maybe she needed to be disappeared.

Today was no different.

Yuki wandered in quietly, her eyes on her bare toes, which dragged across the floor as she barely lifted each foot. Chala hung by a leg, the rest of her limbs flopping. Yuki had moped all the way from the Lower Market, shadowed by a castle guard, making a game of tearing at the tough skin of her feet with the gritty sand. *Even* scrapes, she told herself. Every step should sound the *same*. Scuffle, scuffle, scuffle. Her focus was so intent upon her game that it took her a moment to recognize the pleasant melody of Mother's encouraging voice interspersed with Kei's faltering reading.

Kei was smart, like Tai. She had books without pictures in them, like the one she was reading from now. Its slightly yellowed pages fell across her lap, riddled in line after line of flowing Shiggon-jin script. Not a single drawing. "This event was the . . . the initiation of the greatest ma . . . massacre of myrkind. Those without godly form called it a cleansing—" She stopped short and glanced at Yuki.

Mother started from her needlework as though she had pricked her finger, her expression clouding and closing, and then she smiled proudly at Kei. "Well done, Kei-sho. That's enough for today; we'll continue tomorrow." She neatly folded the cloth in her lap, placing the needle and spare thread inside. "Taiuki, you're filthy again. I can smell the fried oil on your clothing. Nurse, do give her a bath." She rose, taking baby Tan from Nurse's lap, and glided out of the room.

"Yes, my queen." Nurse remained with both palms to her face, fingertips touching the center between her brow, until Mother was gone, then set a pot of water to boil over the fire.

Kei clapped the book shut with a satisfied preen, exchanging it for a hairbrush. She frowned as the brush immediately caught in her hair beads. "Nurse, take these out now."

Yuki offered her help and began brushing her sister's wavy black locks, admiring everything she saw. Kei was pretty with her makeup and her colorful dresses and her wider, more expressive eyes, and she was refined like Mother. Always holding her shoulders back and her chin high, always moving gracefully.

"What were you reading?" Yuki asked.

"A history. Master Merridan gave it to me," Kei replied. "It's too advanced for you."

"Will you read me something before we go to sleep?"

"Sure— Ouch!" Kei glared at Yuki. "Be careful. I'm not your stupid doll."

"Sorry." Yuki tried harder. "You look really nice. Where were you today? The garrison?"

"Do I look like I was at the garrison?" Kei snapped. She shook her head slightly and rolled her eyes at her own reflection.

Yuki scanned her sister again. Kei wore an elaborate skirt, asymmetrically cut to trail long behind her and layered with multiple silks. The embroidered edges shone with beads and stitching, and her tunic had flaring ruched sleeves to match the skirt. Over that, she wore a decorative scale-pattern vest rather than mail armor like she used to. She even had a long silky cape, which now hung over the chair back.

Kei eyed her. "Still trying to figure it out? Wow. No, I don't have time to be there anymore."

The way she said it made Yuki think she didn't care all that much, but Kei had been training in the garrison since before she was Yuki's age. Almost every day was spent at the training hall or in the War Room with their uncle, Arch Commodore Sashiro.

"Why?" The question came from Yuki's lips, and she immediately regretted it because Kei snapped at her again and battered her brushing hand away.

"Because now I have to be at court, with Father. Why do you think?"

"Oh." The room grew quiet other than the sounds of Nurse pouring hot water into the bath. Yuki sighed. Kei had to give up her training in order to fill Tai's position as First. *That* was why she wasn't at the garrison anymore. She must have been sad about it, no longer having lessons with their uncle or getting to practice fighting. Plus, court was boring.

Tai had been really good at all of that stuff, shadowing Father and making wise decisions about citizen hearings and tariffs—all things Yuki thought were very dull.

She wrung her hands around the hairbrush handle and stared at her sandy, scraped-up feet. "I miss Tai. Don't you?"

The question hung in the air for a long minute, and then Kei slowly spun in the chair to face Yuki. Her eyes sparkled with moisture, and her flat visage twisted into a nasty scowl.

"Of course I miss him."

Her words were acid, delivered in a dangerously soft, low voice, and Yuki flushed. "Do you . . . do you think he misses us too?" There was life after this, right? The god I'ya watched over souls when they passed through to the next Gate, and sent them somewhere nice. When they entered the current, that was where they went.

"He's dead." Kei delivered that brief statement with such finality that Yuki would have thought she was done speaking for the rest of the night. But then she yanked the hairbrush from Yuki's loose grip and spun around to face the mirror and examine herself. "Thanks to you," she added.

Yuki froze. Her breath stopped in her chest, and again she felt like she was falling, suffocating, the world closing in around her as her body struggled in vain for sustenance. Her cheeks burned, her forehead burned, her heart clenched like a soldier's gauntleted fist.

What did Kei mean?

"He wouldn't have gone in if *you* hadn't started that fight. He was smarter than that." Kei's voice trembled. The wetness in the corners of her eyes finally overflowed onto her cheeks, just like Yuki's, or perhaps even worse because her sister *never* cried. Yuki had done something terrible to make her weep. Kei yanked the brush through her own hair, and Yuki could hear the snapping and breakage of her fine black strands. Then the brush caught on a string of beads Nurse had missed. Kei screeched her frustration. She threw the brush at the mirror, and it shattered to pieces all over the vanity. Ignoring the crashing sound and the sharp mess completely, she stood and towered over Yuki. Although Yuki cringed back, Kei leaned into her face, closer and closer. "It's your fault, Yuki. It's your fault he died, and I will *never* forgive you."

Then she turned and climbed into her bed, pulling the sheets high and facing away.

Yuki stood there, dumbly processing the accusation. She barely blinked as Nurse hurried about picking up glass, then undressed her and lifted her into the warm bathwater. She didn't really feel her hair being scrubbed clean or roughly dried, although she was aware of the jolting motion of the world around her. She knew a nightshift of lavender silk was slipped over her head, her skinny arms shoved through the arm openings, but she didn't feel the softness of the material or the yanking pop as a button caught her hair and ripped it out in a small, twisted bunch. She didn't comprehend Nurse apologizing profusely or feel her kissing the sore spot on her head, nor the sensation of being tucked into bed.

She stared into the dark corners of the room for what seemed an eternity. Nurse's presence was gone, and Kei slept. Yuki battled her understanding of her sister's cruel words.

Cruel, yes, but . . . true. True words.

It's your fault, Yuki.

When she finally succumbed to the exhaustion of continual horror, the nightmares were of Tai.

6

Yuki was still drowning, but the weight on her chest had changed somehow.

Her ribs, no longer physically aching, seemed paralyzed, unable to draw outward and inward in the rhythm necessary for life. She felt utterly still, as though her own body were the only stable thing in the world that whirled around her. Sometimes images would come into focus, and she would interact with Nurse or Master Merridan for a moment, and then the moment would fade to a miserable blur.

Sometimes she awoke from those hazy wanderings and found herself in a new place, faltering along the mainway in a daze or staring intensely at nothing near one of the portals.

It's your fault, Yuki.

The echo never stopped, and yet she was the only one who could hear it.

Nurse or a guard seemed to always be there, just out of focus, lingering somewhere in the shadows behind her.

She paused as a litany of squeaks and chirps reached her ears, and she realized she was near one of the parks, a long, low, open cavern with a string of shallow pools and sandy paths and carved statues. Friendly chatter intermixed with the chirps and whines of waterdogs who played in the public area, chasing each other and harassing the tiny crabs who scrambled between pools.

Yuki staggered to a nearby bench and stared.

The pond beyond her feet sang with color, stocked with anemones and corals and small fish. A mother waterdog with a sparkling collar floated on her back in the middle, a small pup on her belly. Two others swam around her, scratching at her side and then wandering off to explore. Yuki watched them play for a while, unaware of a person standing nearby until their intrusive commentary broke through the thudding in her ears.

". . . Highness? They're purebred Nagawan."

She blinked. "What?"

"I have their lineage traced back twelve generations, Your Highness. Good quality, worthy of a princess." The person touched their forehead in a sign of respect. "I heard you liked waterdogs, and there's no better line in Shiggo than mine. No charge, of course. I'd be proud to see one of my pups in the royal home."

Yuki felt her head bob in understanding, but the breeder's words washed over her nonsensically. She *did* like waterdogs. Tai had wanted to teach one to fetch and do tricks, and she had wanted to get it a fancy, jeweled collar and train it to hunt . . . She fell into staring at the mother again.

The creature picked at her pup's fur, scanning and checking for imperfections and parasites. The pup nestled into her, secure and content. Its whines were soft and happy. Something about the scene made Yuki want to cry, and she heard the breeder asking what was wrong. She ignored them and got to her unsteady feet. She needed to get away, right now.

She ran.

The world milled beneath her feet, flying by her and beneath her.

She passed children playing to her left, an elderly man tossing chunks of bread on the right, couples walking with fingers intertwined on the bridge. The park was soon left behind and she was in a hallway once again, streaking by openings and passages and homes. She didn't stop until she tripped and tumbled down a stairwell, landing in a heap at the bottom.

Yuki clutched at the scrape on her knee and whimpered, but the tears didn't come. She didn't want to cry, didn't want to need to cry. Crying meant acknowledgment.

"Oh my, dearie . . ." Nurse's face was in hers, too close, too intense. The woman's tight smile emphasized her dimples, and the concern in her graying eyes was overwhelming.

Yuki looked away and winced, taking in the pain throbbing in her knee. If she allowed that to consume her, she could avoid the temptation to let her eyes water.

"Dearie, it's all right. We'll get you patched up."

Yuki felt herself being gathered into warm arms, a shamble of bones and weakness, and she groaned out her resistance. Chala was on the floor beyond her reach, flopped over herself and covered in sand. She stretched toward the doll, her skinny legs and arms splaying in all directions as Nurse strove to hold her.

The woman bent back down with a huff of effort, and Yuki snatched the doll into her arms. Nurse began to lumber back up the stairs. "There now, let's get you back to the castle. Enough exploring for the day, don't you think?"

"Blood for blood," Yuki whispered mechanically as she examined her dirty doll. Chala was as filthy as she, sand grit stuck in her hair and her dress slightly abraded.

"What's that, dearie?"

"Master Merridan says 'only blood can repay blood,'" Yuki repeated. Her knee throbbed with each of Nurse's steps. Was it enough payment? No. It wasn't.

Nurse looked down at her, emphasizing the looseness of her chin. "My little blade of sweetgrass, you don't need to worry about that yet. Not yet." She squeezed Yuki tighter, and for a moment Yuki thought of the waterdog mother clutching her pup.

She didn't say anything else, instead allowing Nurse to carry her the long way back to the castle in silence. Her knee pulsed with pain, and she became aware that her elbow hurt too. The bright blood welling at the surface of her scrapes slowly darkened and thickened as she watched impassively. She deserved it.

Nurse cleaned her wounds and then washed Chala, returning the doll as good as new with an encouraging smile. "Don't run off like that, dearie, and don't take those stairs two at a time." *But Tai always did.* "I know it's been difficult for you, Yuki-sho, but you must try to let him go with the current."

Yuki sobbed once, then bit the feelings back. Instead, she squeezed Chala as hard as she could without allowing Nurse to see. Her lip pouted out as she looked at her caregiver. "I can't. Everyone else has forgotten him."

Nurse clicked her tongue and gathered Yuki into her arms, rocking her side to side. "No one has forgotten, Yuki-sho."

"But he didn't even get a funeral."

She didn't answer, instead continuing her comforting rhythm back and forth.

Tai hadn't gotten a proper burial. There was nothing to send off in the current, but Kei said that wasn't the reason. Kei said Mother couldn't bear to do the ritual and had refused to allow it to happen. Tai wouldn't get a funeral, and no one would speak his name aloud again. It was forbidden by royal decree.

"I don't want to forget him," Yuki said softly, finally relinquishing control over her tears. "I don't want him to drift away." She thought of the whale disappearing into the blue and wiped her tears with a sleeve, smearing the wet across her cheek.

Nurse held her close and rocked her quietly, allowing her to cry, allowing the surge of repressed horror to well upward and outward. And when Yuki had stopped shuddering and sobbing, and her nose had ceased running, Nurse pushed her back and looked her in the eye.

The old woman gently cupped her chin and gave her a tragic smile. "Father Mana Loi will hold Tai-sho in his arms forever. It may not be the way we wanted things to happen, but we can't change it now. If you want to be near Tai-sho, you must return to the sea and be one with the Water."

A torrent of feelings crashed down upon Yuki: resentment, crippling fear, anger. She pulled away from Nurse and ran, barely conscious of the woman calling after her.

"You mustn't be afraid, dearie. You mustn't be afraid!"

Fear was all she knew. The water yawned in front of her, behind her, all around her, and it tasted like death.

Yuki jolted from her nightmare again, the damp of her sweat making her dreams of drowning all the more eerie and real. Her sheets were wet, and she whimpered when she realized she had wet the bed again. Kei would make fun of her.

As quietly as she could, she yanked the furs from her bed and dragged them to the hallway, then slumped beside the messy pile.

It was the middle of the night. The castle was empty save for the few guards scattered up and down the long hallway, standing stock still beside the lamps, which cast orange circles of light. None of them glanced at her; they were stiff at attention as they were supposed to be.

She pulled her knees in and struggled to control her breathing. Her nightdress was soiled too, and she realized she'd have to return to the room to get a change of clothes. She did so, sneaking by Kei's drowsy form with all the stealth she had, then eloped to the faint night sounds of water trickling and popping.

Although she couldn't leave the castle proper at night, she could wander within, and she did. Her bare feet slipped down the hallway in silence. She retraced all the steps she remembered with Tai, the hopscotch they had played down the unevenly cut stones of the east gallery, the big leaps across the central runner in the long back hall, the heavy landings as they descended to the old dungeons two steps at a time. Tai could go back *up* two at a time too, but she couldn't do that yet.

Yuki expelled a loud gasp as she planted both feet at the bottom of the stairwell. The impact hurt her feet a little, and her knees wobbled for a moment as she gained her balance. Ahead, the old dungeon was dank and unkempt. No prisoners were held here, and so no soldiers were posted. The walls were damp and slimy with the salt-loving wetmold that filled the cracks and crevices. The corners were dark—no lamp burned save for the one at the top of the stairs.

She listened.

The subtle scrape of pestilent crabs touched her ears, a startled scurrying as they noticed the unexpected visitor.

Yuki breathed it in.

The musty odor of abandoned rooms, the wetness of standing water, the sharpness of rusty metal.

A few more steps forward took her into the darkness, and she fell to her knees.

Here along the stone wall, she and Tai had rested after exploring the empty rooms and marveling at the frightening shackles and ropes that had once held criminals in place. She had pulled out her waxy crayons and scrawled a picture of a shark on the wall while Tai told her a scary story.

She traced the faint lines with a finger. The shark image was still there, swimming along the carved granite sea in scribbled yellows and greens—she hadn't had the right crayons that day, but that was okay. And then the lines blurred, and she realized she was crying again.

Unable to pull away from the picture, she tucked her knobby knees back close once again, then slumped down to the floor and stared at it sideways. The vicious monster had its toothy mouth open as it swam through eternity. She could almost see it swaying left to right, cutting through the ocean in a smooth, intent glide.

Exhausted, she allowed her eyes to drift shut, then snapped awake again for fear of nightmares. But every time she blinked her eyes open, they spied the shark image anew, refreshing her mind with wretched thoughts and memories. The monster harassed her awake and in dreams, the shark that killed Tai. Her shark.

It's your fault, Yuki.

She remained where she was, shoulder soaked in a shallow salty puddle on the floor, hair mussed to one side as she lay in a ball on the cold stone. She deserved nothing else.

Her lids finally shuttered all the way closed, heavy with fatigue, and she slept.

"Please, Yuki-sho, at least try." Master Merridan rubbed his temple with one hand.

She stubbornly refused.

No amount of cajoling, bribing, or yelling would convince her to immerse herself in the water again. She knew she would drown, just like before, and everything in her body resisted the risk.

Every part of her wanted to run, which was why Master Merridan had been forced to keep the door shut during her lessons.

The Waterpriest knelt in front of her, pleading. "My child, do you not realize who you are? You are the blood of Noriko Tatami. You are powerful, you are strong, you are capable. You are myr of the purest blood, closer to the Most High than anyone else around you. You *can* swim."

She shook her head quickly, and his face fell.

"And you used to talk more," he lamented. "I know you won't remember this, but when you were Tan's age— Yes, I knew you back then too. I cradled you during your christening. When you were first challenged with the shift, you dove in face-first, arms flailing and mouth open. Your toddler's laughter changed to chirps like it had always been meant to be, and we couldn't get you to shift back for two bells." He chuckled lightly and patted her head. "You only came out when Keiki demanded you play with her."

Yuki hung her head. All of it made a strange shame churn in her belly, and she didn't want to think about it anymore. "Please let me go, Master," she said, her voice quiet.

"I cannot, my child. I cannot when I see such potential in you." He stroked her hair in comfort, then cupped both her cheeks and stared at her. "You *must* be one with the Water, to be who you are. Being separate from it is like being cut off from part of yourself. I don't expect you to fully understand this philosophy yet, for you are still a child, but I will never stop telling you this truth."

Yuki couldn't look away. Master Merridan had such a powerful personality, and she had always liked him, even when he forced her to scribe the dry prayers on endless sheets of vellum. His dark eyes were slightly browner than typical, rimmed in obsidian and flecked with sunshine that leaned more toward the pale yellow of the sea stars outside the Kelp Gate. When he laughed, they disappeared, scrunched inside chubby cheeks. His round face featured a fine, thick black beard streaked with silver, much thicker than Uncle Sashiro's. The honorable robes of a Waterpriest draped his rotund body: an indigo cloak over shorter-edged cerulean skirts and a finely tailored leather tunic with decorative golden scales. His long hair was braided with golden and indigo beads that reminded her of Chala, and he wore rings upon rings of golden bracelets upon his wrists. He always smelled of delicious food, and he almost always carried sugar kelp candy in his voluminous pockets.

His friendly smile grew as Yuki maintained eye contact, and he nodded to himself. "See now, no fear. You're not intimidated by me, even though I'm an adult and a Waterpriest. Why would you need to be intimidated by something as innocuous as the water?"

She didn't know what "innocuous" meant, but she thought she knew what he was trying to say. Nevertheless, she couldn't face the water.

He seemed to notice her hardening in her resolve, and he sighed. He turned away to rummage through the teaching scrolls, no doubt to pull out a new set of prayers or some other litany on the Way of the Current, some new attempt to help her understand why she shouldn't be afraid.

Yuki darted for the door and wrenched it open, hearing him shout from behind. She felt a tug on her breechbelt skirting, which fluttered farther behind her than it did in front, and then a tear.

Elated by the small victory, she ran, spurting through the legs of the guards at the castle gate and throwing herself headlong into the crowds on the mainway. She scrambled between people, ducking under arms and squeezing between skirts and capes, leaping over leashed waterdogs, until the castle proper was far behind.

She caught her breath when she reached the Lower Market, a massive cavern seething with trade banter and movement as myrfolk exchanged goods, dried and packaged forage, and prepared fresh food at the endless rows of stalls. Walkways meandered between tightly packed buildings that towered to the ceiling, providing second and even third stories in which the moneycounters presided over their books and counted talons into careful stacks. All walkways led to the Lower Market Gate, which opened to an extensive town, one of many suburbs to Shiggo City.

The Shiggon-jin who lived there were more fish than they were men, spending more time in myrform than they did human. Many were foragers and freemen, hunting the ocean for flesh and fruit and bringing the most incredible items to market, which sold at a high price locally and an even higher price to outsiders. Others were farmers and fishkeepers, and some worked the stables and handled the extensive herds of whales. Still others were soldiers, part of the garrison farther downslope.

In the end, she supposed being a soldier and being a hunter were not all that different. The valiant Shiggon-jin stayed in myrform for long periods, hunting synchronously and taking down vicious predators who posed a risk to the city. Whether those dangers were wild creatures or other myr didn't really matter, in the end. Hunting was hunting.

Yuki scrunched her eyebrows together. Kei had said she no longer went to the garrison, but what did that mean for Yuki? Was *she* the Second now?

She shook the thought away and settled close to the gate, where the number of distractions could keep her occupied.

The people moving through the gate were industrious, moving constantly between the town and the open-air market, shifting fluidly and thoughtlessly as they passed through with their wares. Sometimes they gave her wary glances, but they rarely spoke to her. If they did acknowledge her, it was with a quick touch to their forehead followed by a hurried step. That was a fairly minimal allocation of respect. Perhaps they had heard the dark and frightening rumors that she had nearly drowned, that she was afraid of the water. That she couldn't shift anymore. That she wasn't myr *enough*, inferior now like a landwalking human.

Maybe they all thought she should be disappeared.

She ducked her head in shame and pulled her knees in. Posed like that, she watched and listened, engulfed by the raucous market din. She didn't disagree.

Her favorite part of the day was the noon meal. Traffic would increase in the market as townspeople came in to purchase crusty fish pies and raw fish rolls wrapped in red kelp. Yuki would wander past each stall, Chala in tow, peering at the wares until she found something that piqued her interest. Fried shellfish? No. Crab turnover, smothered in cheese? Blackened oysters in butter? Hmm. She settled on a savenberry turnover and a handful of sugar kelp candies. The vendor bowed deeply, both hands over his face, as she returned to a barrel to sit. The powdery sugar on the turnover covered her lips and dusted her thin shirt. It was so juicy and tart. She was so occupied with the turnover that a candy slipped out of her grasp and fell to the sand as she walked.

Yuki alighted on top of the barrel, high enough that she was able to swing her legs as she munched on her meal. As she did so, she saw a flicker of movement as a crab scuttled out from under a vendor's table, pinched her sand-covered candy, and scurried off. She unclenched her candy-filled hand and realized her error but started giggling when her aggravated huff sent a cloud of powdery sugar onto her chin and shirt.

The little crab could keep her candy.

Now she was paying better attention. Other animals lurked in the corners of the market. Crabs, certainly, were a common pest, scurrying about stealing bits of food and pinching toes under the tablecloths. But there were also waterdogs following their masters through the aisles, blind bats tucked up in the corners of the cavern, and trundling pillworms harassing the sacks of old produce. Beyond the gate, there was far more: starlilies and anemones adorning the rocky facade, tiny frilled shrimp skittering about the edges, hoping for a dropped meal, and sluggish greatworms filtering the detritus from the town. And she caught a subtle movement out of the corner of her eye, a tendril hand slipping out from under a tablecloth, probing the table above.

The tentacle-like arm was beige and smooth-textured like the cloth, and slow-moving. It crept up and gently prodded a tartlet, then wrapped around it. The pie inched closer and closer to the edge, then flipped out of sight under the tablecloth. Yuki sat intrigued as crusty bits fell to the ground under the vendor's table. The man was oblivious, moving about behind his stall as he constructed more pies.

Yuki had finished her turnover and began popping the sweet, salty candies into her mouth. When she had one left, she pondered it for a moment, then tossed it to the ground under the nearby vendor's table. It rolled to a stop next to the bits of pie crust.

After what seemed an eternity, the arm extended from under the tablecloth, creeping along the wooden table leg and down to the sand. It stretched out and picked up the candy, then withdrew once again.

Yuki smiled, an unfamiliar expression after so many weeks. She continued to swing her legs, humming a little to herself as the noon rush faded away.

7

YUKI VISITED THE LOWER Market day after day, sometimes early, when the sea smelled of newly opened tanko blooms and rising plankton, and sometimes late, when the impending evening yielded cookfires and hot oil and savory scents.

Nurse had insisted on bathing her again when she returned home covered in sugar, her hands and face sticky, and had guessed where she was thereafter. Nonetheless, the old woman rarely gave away Yuki's location to Merridan, saving Yuki from an endless litany of lessons. It was a large market after all, lots of nooks for a small child, and Yuki was a particularly elusive little girl. She could run faster and farther than Master Merridan, and no one could stop her. She was, after all, a princess of Shiggo.

Merridan stared severely at Yuki now, his salt-and-peppered eyebrows drawn together, frown lincs tugging at the corners of his mouth. He had said something important, something he wanted her to hear and remember. Yuki nodded an affirmation.

The Waterpriest sighed, and his shoulders slumped. "No, my child, the water is not to be feared! How many times did you swim before? How many times did you shift to the higher form? Countless already in your young life. The form is within you, a part of you; it must be for it already was. Recite the Way," he instructed. "Then recite it again."

Yuki huffed but obeyed. "The *myr* are one with the Water . . ."

It seemed hours later when Merridan allowed her to leave. He had forced her to immerse herself in a long tub of water, and the time had swirled around her in a muddle of nerves and chaos. She had failed to shift again, and again, and again, and now she slipped away to hide, shaking at the knees with fury and frustration.

How could she shift? Every time she considered it, she saw Tai's silent scream, and she remembered how she couldn't save him. She remembered that she had caused it all, by shifting and showing off to people who didn't even matter. People who weren't even people, whose opinions didn't matter. Tai had stepped up to defend her honor and that of the myr.

She plopped down in a corner close to the Lower Market Gate and pulled her knees up to her chin, scanning for the octopus. It wasn't a proper way of sitting, giving her skirting, but she didn't care. She was hardly a myrperson and didn't belong anyway.

Tucked under a table, squeezed into a crack in a barrel, or perhaps camouflaged at the gate's edge, the octopus was a daily visitor, particularly around mealtimes. She didn't always find it, but the game was entertaining enough to keep her looking. Sometimes, when it had been out of water for a while, it would slip into a barrel of fish and emerge refreshed, the fishmonger none the wiser. Today, she spotted it emerging from the barrel and slithering quickly under an adjacent table to hide.

Yuki happily got up and visited a stall to get food. This time, she got baby scallops and another handful of candy. The octopus loved scallops. And candy. Yuki installed herself near the table, facing the street, and inconspicuously tossed a scallop under the table. The tendrils reached out and pulled the morsel into the shadows. She tossed another, then another, then another. Each nugget was carefully embraced and eaten. The last scallop gone, Yuki gently flicked a candy under the table. She overshot, and it rolled a little farther away than she had meant it to.

The octopus slowly reached out to take it, uncurling a tendril arm outward and stretching thin and long.

"Hey!" A vendor across the walkway shouted. He pointed below the table. "Octopus!"

In an instant, the fishmonger grabbed a knife and knelt below the table, reaching under the cloth. He emerged grasping a writhing, flashing mass of twisting arms. He slammed the creature on his workbench, preparing for a clean stab to the head.

Yuki cried out.

The walkway quieted for a moment. Several vendors, including the fishmonger, stared strangely at Yuki as she ran up to the larger man.

"Please don't." Tears burned a path down her cheeks. "Please . . . he's my friend."

The fishmonger set his knife on the table but kept a firm grip on the squirming creature. "They bite, Your Highness."

Yuki held out her hands. "Please."

"They are pests."

She raised her gaze to him and pouted, then scowled as she had seen Tai do when he wanted something.

The man shook his head in confusion, but after hesitating another moment nonetheless handed the angry creature over with his lip curled in disgust. He touched his brow with his free hand. "Take care, Highness."

The animal wrapped itself tightly around Yuki's arm, twisting about and up until it had tucked itself in her armpit. Yuki squealed a little, and her panicked breath caught in her chest. Then, feeling the weight of scrutiny upon her, she scurried out of the market, the octopus in tow.

Yuki ran until she was out of breath, the one arm flailing loosely so she didn't crush her new friend. She flew down the mainway, jumping stairs three at a time and nearly losing her footing, and passed the Garrison Gate to one of the quieter portals. She careened down the side hall, leaving the mainway and turning a corner to face the vertical wall of water. The cavern shimmered with an angle of light from above that lent a blue cast to everything.

No one came down this way. Perhaps it would be safe.

She finally stopped, panting hard, and tried to extricate the creature from her shoulder. It wouldn't budge.

Yuki tried to calm herself and knelt in front of the portal, faced with a vast, empty space of dark blue water. This was deeper than the other gates. There wasn't much of a village beyond; it was mostly foragers and hunters living in scattered homesteads. Save for the constant underlying rush of water, an eternal undertone to Shiggo City, it was utterly silent.

Hoping to distract herself from the uncomfortable tightness around her shoulder and arm, she traced pictures in the sand with her free hand. An oval for the head, long squiggly lines for the legs, circles for suckers . . . She subconsciously began to hum a tune from Songmaster Haupan, a sad one. She didn't know all the words, but the melody was pretty. In the emptiness of the gate, her soft sounds seemed to amplify, harmonizing with themselves.

The octopus loosened its grip, eventually peeking out to study her.

She paused sketching to meet its gaze. Face-to-face, the creature seemed to see right into her without judgment. Its fearful scarlet color reduced to a light brown, and it finally slithered out of her armpit and along her arm, stopping at her clenched fist.

She still had candy, now likely crushed into a sticky mass of sweet kelp. She resisted groaning at the ruined treats.

With more strength than she expected, the octopus wrenched her hand open, its tiny suction cups leaving a rash of rings on her skin, and munched the rest of the candy in her palm. When it had finished, it seemed to scan the rest of her hand and then inspect her. Its eyes were fascinating, slitted in an odd direction and surprisingly expressive. Was it evaluating her as much as she was evaluating it? Did it see her broken myrform, or her broken heart? Did it know she was a little girl?

Yuki scooched closer to the gate and held the octopus up to the edge of the water.

"Go on, it's safe now," she said.

With one more penetrating look at her, the octopus pushed into the ocean portal and, stretching its arms wide, propelled away, disappearing into the blue beyond.

Chala's beaded braids clacked together as Yuki turned her upside down, pouring the gravel stuffing out of the doll's body. Chala would make a perfect vessel for transporting food without drawing attention.

Since the octopus had been discovered, Yuki had daily scoured the corners of the market, hopeful of finding it again. But the octopus had not reappeared.

Maybe it was scared, and by now it was surely starving. So today, she would take some food and see if it was at the quieter portal.

"What are you doing?" Kei's irritation cut into her peaceful thoughts.

Yuki controlled a gasp of surprise, for she had been so focused on dismantling Chala that she hadn't noticed her sister's entry. She was found out. She tightened her mouth into an innocent look, a clueless one that Kei would believe. "Nothing. Playing."

"Well, you're making a mess." Kei tread gingerly across the messy floor, lifting the trailing edge of her skirts as though the gravel were something dirty. She settled in front of the new mirror, where she examined her wavy hair and slicked strays into place. She affixed a showy hairpin to one side. "I thought that was your favorite doll."

Yuki stared hard at the floor. Kei wouldn't understand. She didn't like octopus any more than anyone else did—she thought they were pests, garbage-eaters. Just like the fishmonger at the market, she would react with revulsion and hatred.

Yuki picked at Chala's beads. "She *is* my favorite."

"Then why are you ripping her apart? Mama's going to be upset, you've made such a mess. You do understand we walk on this floor? Now someone has to clean it up, but I think you should have to do it. We have servants for these things, but you're barely better than them." Kei readjusted the hairpin just so, then smiled primly into the mirror before turning toward Yuki. "Not that any of it matters. Mama's already upset with you."

Yuki didn't respond at first, recognizing the cruelty in Kei's disdainful smile and tone. She didn't used to talk that way, but that was *before*.

Yuki puzzled through the words. Mother and Father had hardly been around lately. Father was busy ruling the kingdom, entertaining requests for judgment and making laws and establishing taxes, and Mother was busy with Tan-sho. Why would they be upset with her?

"Because you're a weak landwalker who can't swim, not to mention a little slow in the head." Kei smirked. "You're such an embarrassment, Yuki. I don't understand how we can be related. Unable to do the one thing that everyone can do, afraid of the water, afraid of everything. The only thing you're good at is running away from things that scare you. Myr don't run. Shiggon-jin don't run. You probably should have been disappeared."

Yuki's stomach twisted into a new knot. For weeks, she had known only guilt and fear, but now she felt something new. Rage.

She grabbed a handful of gravel and threw it in Kei's face.

With a surprised yelp, her sister flinched, then slapped Yuki so hard she fell backward. Gravel skittered everywhere, and her elbows scraped raw.

Kei suddenly loomed over her. She flicked bits of gravel out of her hair with a disgusted sneer, then struck Yuki again on the other cheek. "You're not Tatami. You're a freak. You're just a landwalker, and when I am queen, I'm going to make you go live on the surface with all the other landwalkers. You don't belong here with real people." She stepped over Yuki and strutted out with one last flip of her silky hair, leaving Yuki in a heap of teary-eyed bones.

She curled into a tight ball and cried for a while on the bumpy floor. The stones from Chala's insides felt cold on her skin, cold and smooth. She held the doll, now a loose shell with floppy arms and legs, tight against her chest. Her elbows stung, and her cheeks burned and flared with heat. She wasn't *really* a landwalker, was she?

Doubt filled her. Myr were gifted by Water through the blood, and she came from the bloodline of Shiggon-jin kings and queens just as her sister did. But magic wasn't always predictable. Maybe her gift had been taken away, a penance for causing Tai's death. Blood for blood, like Master Merridan said. That would make sense.

Kei was right. She was older and smarter, so she knew about these things.

Finally sitting up, Yuki shook the last of the gravel bits out of Chala's body and made a nice sack, then scurried to the Lower Market. When she had stuffed the doll full with oysters and candy, she retreated to the other portal where she had last seen the octopus.

With nothing better to do than sulk, she waited in patient silence.

An eternity passed, with occasional passersby glancing at her as they moved between the public mainway and the houses beyond. No one spoke to her, although they touched their foreheads when they realized who she was. She didn't care whether they saluted or not. She was too busy staring intensely at the gate to pay them any mind.

At last a brown lump appeared on the rocks beyond the gate, then advanced right to the edge of the vertical face of water. It briefly paused, then emerged, slithering its way to Yuki and right up her arm.

She laughed despite her nerves and pulled an oyster from her doll-bag.

The octopus grabbed it, enveloping it until a sharp crack echoed through the chamber. Two half-shells were discarded moments later, and the octopus reached out again. Yuki was ready with another oyster. They continued this way until the doll was empty. Yuki's laughter was a hiccupping combination of half-sobs and giggles.

"It's all right now," she managed between heaving breaths. "I'll take care of you, even if no one else loves you. I think I'll call you Wen."

The octopus twisted about and examined her carefully, then briefly reached out to her cheek. The suction cups brushed against Yuki's skin, and she noted he was likely a male. That was good, because Wen was a boy's name. Then he slid down to the sand and returned to the gate.

Yuki stared after him with a whisper of happiness pulling at her cheeks. She sniffled.

"I'll be back soon," she whispered to the wall of water.

With a heavy sigh, she resigned herself to her lessons. Merridan was surely looking for her.

8

As expected, Master Merridan did not slacken his efforts. Despite Yuki's constant attempts to evade him, he soldiered on, resolute that she recover and obstinate in his faith in her abilities.

He engaged others in his plan to reeducate Yuki; she now shared lessons with her baby brother. Merridan shifted his teachings to the most basic level, passing over poetry and verse for rudimentary repeated drills and nursery rhymes. As a toddler, Tan-sho was ready to swim, perhaps even more so than he was ready to walk. He had a natural inclination to shift at least his toes, needing only a little encouragement to complete the process under supervision. He understood little scripture, nor could he repeat it. But he was myr, and that was enough.

Thankfully, sharing lessons with Tan meant Mother would often attend. She would enter bouncing Tan on her hip, deposit him near Merridan, then sweep to a finely upholstered chair or couch where she could lounge in her beautiful dresses. She was attentive, her obsidian-black eyes sharp, taking in every tiny bit of progress displayed by her children.

It made Yuki want to try harder, to scale the walls of fear that bound her into human form. Consciously, she began to try, although everything in her body resisted.

It was like swimming through a bog, a mire of feelings that drained her vitality. When she failed, again and again, Mother's expression would close. Her pretty red lips would tighten, her narrow eyes squinting until her lashes seemed to touch each other, and a light furrow would wrinkle her otherwise smooth, flat forehead. And then she seemed to let it go, easing back with a sip of her wine and turning her focus to Tan with an adoring smile. If only she would turn that adoration toward Yuki.

Yuki had to try harder.

Merridan's first drills focused on nonvital changes in the inner ear. These changes were natural to myr. In the ear, the pressure of impending water was usually enough to force the body to adjust, equalizing the air inside and out subconsciously. With her ear to the surface of a vertical wall of water, Yuki would sit and listen, straining to hear the Waterpriest clearly on the other side and praying the unpleasant push on her eardrum would go away. Sometimes it did, incrementally, and sometimes it didn't. Sometimes the lack of squeal and pop escalated to a screaming pain, and she cried.

Then Merridan encouraged her to turn to the wall of water, to immerse her face. Again, the shift in the eyes and nose should have been automatic. The nose should have shuttered to a set of finer slits, and the eyes would acclimate to the high salt content of the ocean. The burning sensation, the sting that felt like Fire instead of Water, would recede, and the vision would clear.

This didn't seem to happen, and Yuki would face the blurry wall as long as she could before running out of breath and nerve. The haze reminded her of the day she nearly lost Chala in the current. The sense of drifting into the unknown, into the darkness, the chaos and terror. She couldn't do it.

She fell backward with a sob and rubbed the sting of salt from her red eyes, then ran to Mother's arms. Why couldn't she shift her vision at least? It hurt, not only on the surface but somewhere inside, but it also hurt *not* to.

Mother patted her shoulder with one hand while holding her wine glass aloft with the other, and then her free hand found Yuki's hair and stroked it once with trembling fingers. Yuki exulted in the brief moment of comfort, but it didn't last.

A soldier rushed into the room and dropped to his knees with a two-handed salute, both palms covering his eyes. "My queen," he gasped.

Mother pushed Yuki back and beckoned for her to return to Master Merridan. Yuki half obeyed, taking only a few reluctant steps back while staring at the soldier.

He was a long-range scout, and his breechbelt bore the rankstones of a captain and the colors of a tracker. He still wore a uniform and armor that implied he had just returned from the sea, including a wicked chinespine along his back. The flared spines would make any potential predator think twice before attacking, but he was undoubtedly also a blue shark rider. Blues were the best trackers, able to take nearly any scent and pursue it to the ends of the ocean.

"Report," Mother commanded.

The scout remained on his knees, his gaze averted to the feet of Mother's couch in deference, but he did drop his salute before speaking. "Your Highness, my hunters report there is still no sighting of the beast, but we did pick up a suspicious trail. We're searching deeper to the south and west now. Several whale pods have passed by recently, and one from the south seemed especially agitated."

Mother took a deep, slow breath in through her nose, her expression almost frozen as she listened. Then she flicked a hand at the scout in dismissal. "Continue searching, Captain, and recruit an additional team if you need to. Find it. The king and I would prefer it returned alive if possible."

The soldier touched his forehead again. "I shall conform, Your Highness." He rose and departed.

Yuki stared out the door, then back toward Mother's feet. She spied her expressions in her peripheral vision.

Mother's face had hardened once again, and she seemed distracted.

It was the beast they were looking for. The monster that killed Tai.

Mother didn't *only* want it dead. She wanted to take its life herself, with Father by her side. Perhaps she even wanted to torture it. (Yuki had heard of that, although she didn't understand what it really meant.) Together they would punish the monster who stole away Shiggo's First son.

I will never forgive you, whispered Kei from somewhere inside. *It was your fault.*

A new idea sparked in Yuki's mind, crackling like lightning in a tumultuous black thunderstorm in summer, violent like an explosive potion.

Kill it, and maybe you can redeem yourself. Water for Water, Blood for Blood.

And suddenly Master Merridan's lessons made sense.

Yuki could seek out the beast herself and try to kill it, for Tai, for Mother, for Kei, for Father. For them, she would do anything. Whatever was required. Ol Shiggo'lo, *all* for Shiggo. She could shove a spear through its brain like she had seen the soldiers do. She could hammer its side with harpoons and send bolts into its eyes, and then it would see what death really tasted like.

She *would* learn to swim again, she resolved, pushing away the fear that had nearly consumed her. She would learn to swim, so she could find the monster.

And kill it.

Yuki meandered through the castle, eventually finding her way down a corridor she had long avoided.

On the second underwater level was the War Room, a room in which Tai had spent countless hours with their uncle Sashiro, the arch commodore. The walls were littered with storage: sheaves of maps and routes and histories. Battle theory was documented in sloping Shiggon-jin script on timeless, waterproof vellum sheets, and books filled the shelves in leather bindings.

Upon the floor was a map of the world, a scale model with divots for trenches and peaks for the highest mountains that pushed upward from the sea. The more important land kingdoms were carved in great detail—Krita, Towun—along with the surface-level portions of the myrkingdoms. The detail faded at the edges of the Mana Loi, for the inland features of places like Mirat or Shayal were irrelevant. Yuki stepped around the model with reverence, noting the position of each border and the deployment of border troops.

Her feet shuffled as she considered how Tai's feet had crossed this same spot many weeks before, how they had stomped to the desk beyond. How he had likely bent over a book in deep thought, studious and attentive to all that Sashiro tried to teach him. He would have sat in *that* chair, with a lamp lit and flickering beside him, casting a warm yellow glow across the letters of the pages.

The light would have matched the yellow speckles in his eyes. Tai always had the most colorful eyes, not a common feature among myr since most of the iris was black.

She stared dully at the empty nook. The lamp was snuffed, and the few books were shut and placed upright along the wall, aligned and orderly. Sheets of vellum were stacked neatly in a rectangular pile, and the inkwell was empty.

A hand clamped upon her shoulder, and Yuki wheeled around with a gasp, clutching Chala tightly to her chest. Then she broke into a grin.

"Uncle Sashiro!"

She flung her arms around his waist and clung to him. He stood stiffly, one hand still on her shoulder, then eased her away.

"Decorum, Second."

His deep voice seemed to echo in the emptiness of the war room, and she looked up at him as her cheek left his warm torso. She allowed her arms to loosen and fall to her side, then stood facing him. She should have realized he'd be in his office adjacent, but he was so quiet, and she had been immersed in her own thoughts.

He examined her with a stern expression, looking her up and down and then nodding with seeming satisfaction. "Finally, you've come to claim your place."

Yuki stared at him, eyes wide. What did that mean?

He knelt, meeting her eye to eye. He gently adjusted her shoulders, pushing them back and tipping her chin up, then adjusted each of her feet together with toes angled outward. He uncurled the fingers that clenched a raggedy, floppy Chala and set the doll aside.

"Now you're at a position of attention, Yuki-sho," he said softly. "You'll stand like this when meeting me, and others will stand like this when meeting you."

She lowered her head, shame tugging at her as she thought of Tai, but Sashiro nudged her chin back up again.

A brief, encouraging smile touched his lips, then disappeared. "You're the Second now, Yuki-sho, and I know you will be a strong one. You came here on your own, just as I knew you would."

She stared at his chest, not speaking, and swallowed hard at the lump in her throat. Tears threatened, and she tried to blink them back.

Sashiro spoke. "You shall address me as Arch Commodore or sir, as is proper, and I shall address you as Second or Arch-Commodore-in-Training. You answer to me directly now. Do you understand?"

She started to nod, then stopped herself, instead answering, "I shall conform, sir."

He seemed satisfied with that, standing once again. "Now tell me, Second, why did you come here today? Stay in that position, eyes toward that wall. You mustn't look directly at me unless I give you permission."

Yuki thought for a moment. She thought she had been wandering aimlessly, but she knew that wasn't the truth. "I came to learn, sir," she answered at last.

"And why do you want to learn?"

"So I can kill the beast, sir."

Sashiro tore his eyes from the scale model and looked hard at her, seeming to pierce right through her. He waited, and she waited, until an interminable amount of time lay heavy between them. She capitulated under his stern gaze.

"I want to kill the shark that killed Tai," she managed, her voice breaking. "I want blood for blood, sir." The tears finally broke from their prison, streaming down her flat cheeks.

Sashiro watched her quietly, then removed a perfectly folded kerchief from his chest pocket and approached to dab her face.

Yuki strove to stay at attention, squeezing the last of her tears out and then blinking rapidly. She kept her gaze on the far wall as instructed.

Her uncle knelt once again and caught her eye. "You are right to pursue blood for blood, Second, but not for vengeance and not in anger. You must pursue it in the name of justice, of righteous balance in the world, and you must do so with unflappable comport."

She didn't understand half of those words.

Sashiro continued. "It is the Way of the Current to seek equity in what is given and what is taken away. As arch commodore one day, you will have to make the difficult decisions regarding this give-and-take. If blood is spilled by another, then their blood must be spilled. And if you take a life, you are liable for the results."

Yuki struggled to take his words in, to brand them upon her heart as a permanent lesson, but it was difficult to sear a new memory on something that was in pieces.

It's your fault, Yuki.

The intrusive thoughts never stopped.

Sashiro carefully folded his handkerchief and returned it to his pocket, the corner sticking out at a perfect angle. Then he looked at her for a long time. He adjusted her feet again and squeezed both her shoulders. "Now you're at ease."

He stood once more and paced to the scale model, stroking his long, narrow beard. Two long braids hung from the corners of his mustache, and one jutted from his chin. The one on his chin was decorated with blue beads and pearls.

Finally, he spoke. "It is well you've come, for your duties as arch-commodore-in-training should begin as soon as possible. That said, it is not your responsibility to kill the beast. I have several teams searching for it to the south and west, along this trench and this grassy plain, even through the deeper areas. And when we find it, we will bring it to your father, the king, that he may take reparations as he sees fit. He lost his son and heir, and he above all deserves to rebalance the scales in the name of all Shiggon-jin."

"Yes, sir." Yuki's mind was screaming, confused, frustrated. She wanted to be the one who made it right. She needed to be. Why else overcome her fear?

She snuck a glance at her uncle. He was a reasonable man. Maybe if she proved how capable she was, he would change his mind. He assumed Father would want to kill the shark, but wouldn't Father be even more gratified if she killed it *for* him in Tai's name? Wouldn't Mother be proud of her again? Maybe Kei would even forgive her.

He was wrong. It was her responsibility to kill the monster. She would figure out how to swim again, and she would learn to fight, and she would learn how to use every weapon so that she could take the battle to that creature and to every other thing that threatened Shiggo. She would be the best Second that Shiggo had ever seen, his protege and eventually his replacement.

She returned her gaze to the wall just in time.

Sashiro nodded toward her. "Now that you're ready, come to me every afternoon to study, after your lessons with Master Merridan. Listen closely to his words, and work hard. When you've achieved the shift, we'll move our training to the garrison as well. I will teach you all you need to know."

"I shall conform, sir."

"Carry on then, Second." He dismissed her, and she stooped to pick up Chala. As she passed her uncle on the way out, he reached out and placed his palm on her cheek. He gave her a tight, sad smile so fleeting, she could have imagined it. Then he gently pushed her toward the door. "Carry on," he repeated.

She touched her forehead in a belated salute and left.

9

Day after day, she tried.

Yuki would succeed no more than once, in some small shift, such as shuttering her nose against the incoming flood of water, before Master Merridan would introduce another more challenging process.

You must be able to see in order to kill it, she told herself, forcing her vision to clear in the salt. The tension in her skinny body was not allowed to be fear. It had to be fury and readiness.

Merridan forced her to shift her eyes back the moment she managed the change, and then he made her shift one eye and one ear, but not the other. It was like winking, which was also hard. (Tai could wink. He always winked with a lopsided grin, usually right before he showed her something new.)

But even as she managed to make the nonvital changes in her head, a series of steps that brought great relief to her struggling body, she failed over and over to form her gills. The very thought made her chest ache and tighten, like being on the edge of a violent hiccup and not having it come. It caused a pain in her ribs on either side, accompanied by a panic attack where the wet world beyond the gates and windows closed in to suffocate her.

But myr don't drown, Yuki.

And the flavor of it. The acidic burn on her open gills . . . She whipped her thoughts away violently, and Master Merridan drew his brows together.

"Don't be angry at yourself, my child. You're doing exceptionally well." He stepped through the vertical wall of water between them and helped her back to her swaying feet.

She had been holding her breath again, pushing herself as near to passing out as she could before tumbling out.

Hot tears instead of salt blurred her vision as she watched Tan crawl back and forth through the wall of water, from one side to the other and back. His giggles shifted to chirps and back to giggles as he trundled along, laughing to himself each time. On the far side of the water wall was Mother, sitting in her chair with a book in hand and a faint smile lighting her face whenever Tan reached her and patted her knee. Then he returned: giggle, chirp, giggle. He tottered to Yuki and hung on her, his round face alight with joy.

"Wa-sho," he declared, tugging on her shirt and pointing at the water. He was giving the water a name of endearment, like a person. He laughed, then turned and staggered through again.

Yuki looked up at Master Merridan biting her lip, desperate for hope. Would she ever be like Tan again, or like Tai? Or was she broken?

Merridan smiled down at her, then waved the wall of water into a long tub. The remainder slipped out the window to rejoin the sea. He picked her up and hugged her tightly for a long moment, then carried her to the tub. "It's all right, Yuki-sho. The gills are a vital change, a significant alteration of not only tissue, but also cell function and circulatory adjustment. How about we work on something a little easier?"

Tan shrieked his disagreement, then toddled over to the high window and pouted at the ocean beyond.

Merridan indicated that Tan's lessons were done for the day, and Mother took him away. He squirmed in her arms to no avail, and she headed to the door on silent bare feet. Her elegant dress train whispered behind her, a marvelous traditional cut complete with a silky cape that linked to her elbows. She was glorious, a queen in every way. So beautiful and commanding. She left without a word.

Yuki watched her disappear with her cheek on Master Merridan's shoulder, feeling the pangs of longing for affection. She clung to him tightly with spindly arms and legs, knowing full well he was going to place her in the tub and work on leg shifting.

He tightened his hold. "Be calm, Yuki-sho. You can do this, but it's okay if you don't do it today. As long as you try, that's all that matters."

She didn't loosen her grip, emulating the way Wen grasped with every limb he had, enjoying the hug as long as Merridan would give it. "I miss Tai," she mumbled into his shoulder.

"I know, dear child. I know." With one more squeeze, he lowered her into the tub, immersing her lower body.

Normally, the immersion would lead to an instinctive melding of the toes, then the legs beneath her breechbelt and skirt. That was what happened with Tan, and what used to happen with her. And as she got older, she had learned she could control it and enjoy baths where she could kick her legs and splash Nurse.

Now, she merely sat, her legs remaining legs and her toes remaining toes. She stuck them out and wriggled them with disappointment.

Master Merridan patted her shoulder. "Don't worry about it, Yuki-sho. We're going to try something new today. You're so focused on your failure, you can't see your own potential. The Water is in you, part of you, and it is only your mind's denial that hinders you. So let's take your mind off it."

He retrieved a history from the table and dragged the chair closer. "Simply close your eyes and listen, my child." He propped the book open against the edge of the tub and began reading.

Yuki had expected another esoteric philosophy from some long-dead scholar, overflowing with flowery words and wisdoms that she didn't really understand.

Instead, it was a study of Queen Noriko, the warrior queen after whom her bloodline was named. Noriko had been Second as well, although she had been born to it properly and had not lost an elder sibling. She hailed from Fumaya, the myrkingdom to the north on the other side of the straits, and she spent her youth skirmishing with petty myrking-doms in the Merchan Sea.

Fumaya had skirmished with Shiggo as well, for they couldn't come to terms regarding the border that twisted its way through the straits, and Noriko nearly killed the Shiggon-jin emissary who forced his way into the castle.

But it wasn't a messenger. It was the Shiggon-jin First, a young man named Kenji, and he carried with him terrible tidings of the fall of Jijito and the siege of Shiggo. He sought sanctuary, for the bulk of his people were not far behind, having abandoned the city with all they could carry. The dreaded Luminaries followed.

Yuki had her arms crossed on the edge of the tub, her chin nestled on her wrist and her eyes glued to Merridan, when the Waterpriest paused. His lips pulled back slowly into a slightly mischievous smile, and his eyes disappeared as his cheeks rose.

"You're doing it, Yuki-sho," he said softly.

She glanced down at her legs. She had been immersed in the story, completely enamored with the blossoming romance of Kenji and Noriko, and she hadn't been thinking about shifting at all.

Her legs were halfway melded together, her toes fanned out and flattening. The scaly texture and smooth fins pushed from her copper skin, shimmering across her as they sought to find permanent placement.

But as soon as she comprehended her own surprise, she thought of Kei holding her back, yanking upon the narrow peduncle to keep her from reaching Tai. Kei had been shouting, her face contorted with effort and . . . was it horror? Yuki had never seen that expression on Kei's face before. Her sister's round eyes had gotten rounder, popping from her skull like a fish, and her entire body had heaved as she dragged Yuki back through the gate. As soon as Yuki moved from the water to the air, Branig's screams had intensified in her ears, an endless wail where the boy never seemed to take a breath.

Yuki shuddered at the memory, and with the involuntary motion came a shiver of rejection. The scales shimmering across her tail faded, and the flaring colors of emerging fins faded to nothing. Her knobby knees reappeared in the conjoined mass, pushing themselves apart once again.

Merridan spoke urgently in her ear. "Don't let go of the magika. Don't be afraid."

But all she could hear were Branig's screams, Kei's sobs, and the awful tearing of flesh and cracking of bones.

She whimpered, kicking her half-formed legs against the tub and leaping over the edge in an awkward tumble. She fell to the floor in a heap, scrambling over herself as her toes and feet struggled to reform.

"Yuki-sho!" Merridan cried, but she was already running.

A guard tried to stop her at the castle gate, and she bit him hard enough to draw blood. The flavor it left on her tongue only made things worse.

She ran until she gasped and coughed, until her ribs ached with every step, until the tough bottoms of her feet felt scathed by the grit of the road. She ran to the quiet gate where Wen had been hiding and skidded to a stop right before hitting the water.

She panted for a while, trying her hardest to control her breath and not allow it to escalate into weeping. *You're the Second now, and officers don't cry.*

How could she still hear Branig when her heart was pounding so loudly? Was there no way to drown it out?

She slumped to the ground, defeated. Maybe there wasn't. Maybe she would hear it forever.

The familiar brown lump shifted among the rocks on the other side of the gate, and before long Wen appeared. He slithered through the gate without hesitation, first crawling up one of her arms, then down the other. He pried open her hands, then did a full circle around her back before coming to rest on her arm once again. He looked at her, entreating.

"Oh, Wen, I didn't bring you anything." She had forgotten Chala in the room. "I'm so sorry. I don't have anything for you today."

Wen stared balefully, turning one of his unique eyes toward her as if reprimanding her. Then he squirted a stream of water.

She huffed, torn between humor and despair, and wiped the water from her cheeks. She stroked him, first on the head and then playing with his wandering arms. It was like a game she would play with Tan, patting hands and clapping. Wen would happily while away the time playing this game until the next bell, if she wanted.

Eventually, Wen slithered down to the ground, but retained one arm curled around her wrist. He drew her forward to the water, tugging, but she re-sisted.

"I can't, Wen-sho," she mumbled.

His colors shifted, going from a ruddy tan to a slightly darker brown with reddish edges.

"I know you're hungry," she answered.

He tugged. He wanted to go hunting? Something in her cracked, and her resolve to be a strong soldier shattered into tears. She wept, her knees sprawled in the sand by the gate and her one wrist pulled through the gate by the insistent Wen. Her wet fingers were splayed out, reaching for a future that wasn't there anymore. She bowed her head, black hair falling to cover her face, and cried.

The tug stopped, and before she knew it, Wen had returned and crawled up her arm, wrapping him-self tightly around her neck in a bizarre hug. He watched her closely, his strange eyes seeming to per-ceive everything, and a set of suckers dabbed at her wet cheeks.

She supposed octopi couldn't cry, so he must have wondered what was leaking from her. No doubt it tasted salty and very ocean-like.

The Water is in you, child. A part of you.

She sniffled and tried to smile, then hugged Wen back, stroking his arms and head. He was so intelligent, so friendly. Maybe he would understand if she explained.

"I can't hunt with you, Wen," she said softly, staring out the portal, "because of something that happened. Something terrible that was my fault. I don't know if I'll ever swim again, even if I try."

Wen loosened his grip, leaving a few suction marks on her shoulder as he moved back to the edge of the water. He watched her.

"My big brother taught me to shift. Did you know that? He was the best swimmer. He taught me how to step through the gates without losing my balance, and he taught me not to be afraid of the big animals that migrate through. He taught me to look harder at everything, and I'd find things that were beautiful. Like you."

Wen seemed to perk up, as though he knew she was talking about him.

"I don't know why people don't like octopus, but I think you're very special," she added. "Tai told me once that it was obvious how intelligent the wild sawtooths were, how you could see in their reactions that they were social and friendly. I see that in you too."

Wen changed colors. It was like current on the sweetgrass fields, shimmering across in waves. Now he was more of a yellow, pebbly hue.

"I'm sorry no one else sees it, but I'll always be your friend."

Wen curled around her wrist again and shuffled through the gate. *Swim with me,* he seemed to say. He tugged, using several other arms to push water.

But she couldn't. The fear and dismay rose up again like bile, and she shook her head. "I can't, Wen. I just can't."

With one more hard look, the octopus released her wrist and eyed her through the gate. She leaned forward, thinking he would give her a tentacled hug, but instead he squirted water in her face again. His gaze twitched across the droplets falling from her chin and hair, almost as if he were laughing, and then he jetted away.

10

Sleeping baby, rest your head,
Precious baby, still your legs,
In your dreaming, find your form,
When you wake, you'll be reborn.

A Shiggon-jin Lullaby

EVERY VISIT WITH WEN forced Yuki to acknowledge her fear. As much as he played in the air-filled chambers near the gates, he wanted her to join him on the other side. He wanted to hunt. He wanted to swim, dancing through the water in an acrobatic motion aligned with the ebb and flow of the current.

Every time his arm twisted around her wrist, she considered following him. She hardened her knotted brow and stiffened her lip, telling herself the feeling in her gut was anger and resolve, not intimidation.

And yet, she couldn't bring herself to pass through, for she was terrified of tasting the ocean again.

What if it tasted like death? Like blood and humors from some creature recently fallen to the feral power of the sea? What if it tasted like Tai's last moments?

And then, in a way that was somehow worse, what if it *didn't*? The once-familiar complexity of salts and minerals and sugar kelp and tanko blooms, washing over her gills and touching the back of her throat, would be a sure sign that Tai was really gone. The beast had left so little of him to mourn, and nothing to bury.

Obedient to the arch commodore's command, she tried as hard as she could to achieve the shift, and bit by bit, she seemed to progress. Master Merridan continued his strategy of distracting her with histories and legends, allowing her body to relax into the form as she marveled at the battles of Noriko and Kenji, the bloody war against Riyogo, and the colonization of the sea makran-infested northwest atolls. Afterward, she would study under Master Sashiro, exploring the reasons behind the failed diplomacy with Riyogo and the differences in crossbow use above and below the surface.

Despite her suddenly busy schedule, she still managed a daily visit to the Lower Market, and then Wen's gate. The market always yielded interesting foods, and Yuki happily tried new options to feed Wen and herself. Once Chala was filled, she would descend to her favorite gate to play with the octopus. Passersby often gave her odd looks, but they would always touch their foreheads and salute when they recognized her.

Beyond accepting their fealty, she ignored them. They didn't appreciate Wen, but she did.

Today, she had found a vendor serving brown eel dusted with spices and grilled on a long white bone. The rich flavor melted in her mouth as she slid each chunk off the skewer. She offered one to Wen, who explored it with a thorough probing and turned it over playfully before shoving it into his mouth.

"You like that one?" She giggled and gave him another piece. She had plenty, for she had grabbed three skewers and crammed them into Chala along with a few pieces of sugar-dusted bread.

She dug for another skewer and gave the entire thing to Wen. His strange eyes seemed to light up at the challenge, and he set to work pulling the chunks off, turning the skewer over again and again.

Yuki couldn't help but laugh, and she pulled a piece of bread out for herself. It was crusty with hot fry oil, gritty with sugar and bits of fried sweet kelp. She tore a big bite off. Wen didn't like bread, so she didn't have to share.

When they had both finished, Wen first crawled inside of Chala to ensure she was empty. He slithered out and sulked.

She shrugged. "I don't have any more, Wen-sho."

He reached out with all his arms and wrapped around her neck.

"By the current—Yuki!" Mother's shriek ricocheted off the walls and portal, echoing through the cavern. Everyone passing by paused and stared at the scene.

Lacking her typical grace, Mother approached from the far end of the cavern, nearly running with a horrified look twisting her features. Kei hurried behind, followed by Nurse.

Yuki dropped Chala in her surprise, and skewers scattered across the floor. She felt Wen tighten his hold as she staggered to her feet.

Mother grabbed her arm and wrenched Wen off. Furious crimson rippled across his limbs, much like the day Yuki had met him, followed by flashes of a pained grayish white. Mother threw him through the gate with a dark expression somewhere between hatred and disgust, then spun Yuki around and shoved her toward Nurse.

"Clean her up. She's filthy." Mother glared at Nurse. "Why didn't you stop her? Why didn't you tell me where she's been hiding and what she was doing?"

Yuki battled to reach toward the gate, toward Wen, but Nurse held her tightly to her breast. Yuki felt her shaking her head as she responded to Mother's accusations. "There didn't seem to be no harm, Highness."

"No harm?" Mother sneered and pointed a long, ring-covered finger at the portal where Wen had disappeared. "These are vermin! Disgusting creatures." She advanced on Nurse until their noses nearly touched.

Yuki stared up at the two women. Nurse's eyes were squeezed shut, and Yuki could feel her body cringing and stiffening.

Mother deliberately wiped her hands clean on Nurse's breechbelt skirting. She glared at Nurse until the woman opened her eyes, then looked down at her feet in shame.

Mother's voice was cold as steel. "I don't want to see her down here again. If I do, you will find new employment outside the castle."

Nurse nodded quickly, and Mother swept away with Kei in tow.

Yuki peeked out from Nurse's embrace, watching her mother disappear. Kei turned back and flashed a triumphant, malicious smile. *I knew you'd screw up,* it said. Then she turned back and hurried after Mother.

With a sinking feeling, Yuki stole a glance at the empty portal. Wen was nowhere to be seen. A shuddering breath escaped her, and Nurse stroked her hair and held her.

"There, there," the older woman murmured. "It's all right now. You did no wrong, Yuki-sho."

Despite her commitment to not crying anymore, Yuki broke into a sob. It wrenched itself out of her violently, clenching her chest and squeezing her stomach. "But I did," she whispered, her voice muffled in Nurse's bosom. "Mother hates me, and Kei hates me. They'll never forgive me because of—because of Tai." She whimpered.

Nurse's embrace was warm and secure, and the woman began rocking from side to side. "No, no, dearie. That wasn't your fault. Is that what you really think? Oh Yuki-sho, no. I know you're here because you want to be closer to him. Isn't that right?"

Yuki sniffled and nodded.

"Then you do whatever you need to do, to let him join the current." Nurse continued to hold her as she began to sing. It was a familiar lullaby, a gentle lilt that matched Nurse's swaying and made Yuki think of quiet winter nights. The notes were soft enough for Yuki's ears alone.

She turned to stare out the gate. It was still, unmarred by the entrance and exit of passersby. The watery world beyond was quiet as well, and Wen was gone.

Yuki missed Wen. His playfulness and curiosity had matched that which she had lost. His bravery—or rather, audacity—to keep coming into the air-filled chambers of Shiggo City for the sake of a spiced scallop or a sweetkelp candy doused in powdered sugar, when he truly belonged in the water, made her giggle.

Although she had resolved to reentering the water to slay the vicious blueback shark, she hadn't wanted to *be* in the water until she met Wen. He reminded her of the elation that came from swimming, being one with the Water instead of the Air.

Since Mother discovered where she played, Yuki had been shadowed by a constant guard, as well as a fluttering, nervously apologetic Nurse. She could hardly wander without someone skulking in the background, ready to redirect her from the Lower Market and Wen's gate. Yuki was confined to the castle proper and the mainway down to the first level, disallowed from going farther without an escort. Even the park, where the waterdogs scampered through the ponds, was off limits unless Nurse had her securely in hand. No one had ever told her where she was and wasn't allowed to go before.

She pouted, but Mother only seemed to care that she progress in her lessons with Master Merridan.

Every day, she rediscovered her abilities, and although a part of her sickened at the thought of shifting completely, another part of her felt a mounting ecstasy. How she craved the taste of Water! How she yearned for the freedom of floating and drifting in the sea, rocked by the ebb and flow of Father Mana

Loi. And how she imagined finding Tai, beckoning her to meet a baby whale or explore a reef . . . although she knew it wasn't possible.

"Wonderful, Yuki-sho," said Master Merridan. "Just wonderful, keep focusing."

Yuki peered between lashes at her legs in the long tub and was surprised to see them conjoined, fusing entirely but out of proportion. Then she squeezed her eyes shut again.

"Now focus on the foot bones, flatter; the spine, longer. Shift."

Yuki invested her entire mind in the drill and felt her body respond. The tissues stretched and changed, her feet flattened to a perfect split fin, and a comforting sensation of *belonging* in the tub of water flowed into her. She was becoming whole again. Almost whole.

Tan clapped his hands and giggled with delight. "Me, me, me!" He bounced with excitement, squirming as Merridan lifted him into the other side of the tub. Tan squealed as his legs became one, and his toes disappeared. He was fast—he reminded Yuki of Tai.

The pair splashed in the water celebrating, but Merridan didn't allow it for long. He made them shift back, again and again, until Yuki was exhausted. Tan was already asleep in Mother's arms when Yuki was released from the drill. Famished, she scarfed an extra serving at supper and slept soundly.

The next day, Master Merridan was busy, so she and Kei followed Mother for morning duties around the castle. This had once been one of Yuki's favorite parts of the day, prancing about in the shadow of her beautiful, noble mother and holding hands with her sister. She and Kei would giggle as they imitated Mother's stern tone and elegant composure.

But Kei no longer held her hand. She said nothing to Yuki during breakfast, drowning her in silence, then remained aloof throughout the morning. It re-minded Yuki of the hollowness of the water when her ears failed to adjust to the pressure, as though a barrier of air blocked the true sound. It was like the terrifying moment as she blindly sought Chala, her body out of balance and her heart pounding like a drum. A thunderous echo in an empty space.

Kei mimicked Mother's grace, her chin high and her shoulders back, the bearing of a queen. Yuki supposed that was good, since Kei was now First and would inherit the crown as soon as she was old enough. But with that haughty bearing, Kei no longer deigned to look down at her, and Yuki sadly wished for the morning duties to simply conclude.

Perhaps she could find Wen and tell him what she had finally achieved, shifting her legs into a long tail, complete with white-edged fins.

Mother released them when she had petitions to hear with Father, and Yuki had until the afternoon before she had to meet the arch commodore.

She sped to her room, where she collected some carved figurines and put them inside Chala's floppy shell. Nurse hurried behind her, and her watchful observation weighed heavy as Yuki wandered the castle looking for the right place to play. Settling on a spot by the buttery, she carefully laid out her toys. A myrman and woman, a whale, several fish, and a ship. Nurse sank into a padded chair in front of the fireplace, although it wasn't lit, and contentedly watched.

The scent of warm yeast and flour exuded from the buttery; the midday meal would be ready soon. Servants popped in and out, allowing the savory flavors of stew and grilled vegetables and fruits to carry on wonderfully warm air. Yuki sniffed it appreciatively, hoping the heat of the ovens would make Nurse sleepy.

The old woman blinked slowly as she watched Yuki play, and then her head slumped to one side. Her tense grip on the armrests eased, and one foot slid outward.

This was Yuki's chance. Noting Nurse's restful appearance from the corner of her eye, she slunk toward the buttery door, abandoning her toys on the ground, then ran.

Servants stepped aside for her, touching their foreheads quickly in deference, and she pumped her legs as she broke from the far door. Through the halls, through the long cavernous rooms, under the guards and out of the castle proper. She flew down the mainway toward Wen's gate, passing soldiers and vendors and people walking their waterdogs. Everyone paused to watch her pass with surprised looks followed by quick salutes of acknowledgment.

She skidded to a stop just short of the water, her nose nearly touching the vertical portal where she had last seen her friend.

"Wen?" She shouted between heaving breaths. "Wen, where are you?"

Her voice seemed to bounce off the walls mockingly (*a thunderous echo in an empty space*) with no reply. Nothing moved beyond the glass-like surface. Where was he? Was he hurt? Was he angry?

"Wen?"

What if Mother had actually injured him? What if she had killed him? Yuki shook her head, rejecting the horrifying thought. Maybe he was just far away. She splashed the portal face with her hands. Wen would often come to the clapping, knowing it was her. But the ocean was quiet beyond the gate. Yuki spotted some townspeople swimming among houses downslope, but no sign of Wen. She willed her heart to slow, and she licked her lips.

Perhaps she should look for him.

The thought stuck like a lump in her throat. Maybe she could show him what her body had finally remembered yesterday, by going *through*. By finding him and taking care of him if he was hurt.

Having finally caught her breath, she touched the gate. The magically maintained surface welled outward briefly, then smoothed. She swirled her fingers in the water, torn between doubt and desire. Then she pushed forward cautiously, focusing hard on shifting her legs, eyes, and ears, and closing her nose.

The salt didn't sting. She forced herself to open her eyes and saw everything clearly: the village and barracks and kelp farms in the distance. Her legs were conjoining into a tail, good.

But her breath didn't come. She winced as panic descended upon her. No air. No air. No air.

She was yanked backward through the portal, falling into Nurse's arms. The woman panted and wheezed, tears coursing down her wrinkled cheeks.

"Oh Yuki-sho, what were you thinking? My poor dear, it's too soon to go alone. Too soon!" She rocked Yuki back and forth.

Yuki shifted her legs and sputtered as she caught her breath. "I wanted to find Wen . . ."

Nurse squeezed her more tightly. "Oh, dearie, of course you did."

"And you didn't stop her." Mother's steely voice cut through the air like a knife—a knife turned upon Nurse.

Yuki and the elderly woman turned to face her together.

Mother glowered, both hands on her hips. An armed guard stood behind her at attention. Both had clearly been running. Mother pointed at Nurse.

"I warned you. You inept, useless woman. Leave. Now."

Yuki felt Nurse's reluctance, the brief squeeze of a hug and the slow release. Nurse pushed her away, ensuring she was balanced on her own two, newly reformed feet before letting her shoulders go. The old woman's loose chin trembled, and she gave Yuki a sad smile as she stepped back.

Nurse raised both hands to her forehead, covering her eyes, and dipped low in a deeply respectful bow toward Mother. "I am so sorry, Your Highness," she said, her voice heavy with shame. "I shall conform."

With that, she stepped backward through the portal, her eyes glued to the sandy floor. Her legs shifted to a grayish tail, and then Nurse was gone.

The next days were momentous, as Merridan pushed Yuki further and faster, making her shift her legs, then her eyes, then both, and finally surrounding her in water until she ran out of breath, forcing her gills to form. She wasn't as frightened now, only angry and bitter.

They were beyond Tan's learning speed and comprehension now, delving into the teaching scrolls as well as practicing, so he played nearby and applied his skills at his own pace, wandering into the wall of water and out again as he chased the rainbows cast upon the floor.

Yuki was on her own. And she could do it, but not without moments of terror when the air ran out. She often held her breath as long as possible. Then, when the world became gray and murky, she desperately sought the final shift. Gills rippled open, and part of her lungs closed. She cried a mouthful of bubbles, still inherently worried the breath wouldn't come, but it did.

She was whole. She was *myr*. Yuki grinned through the water at Master Merridan and clicked her happiness. He smiled and clicked back. Then he released the spell binding the water to her and allowed her to rest.

"You have done well, Yuki-sho. Tomorrow we will practice in the ocean," he said proudly, placing a hand on top of her head and scruffing it lightly. Unlike Tai, though, he didn't ruin her tightly woven braids. "Go on now—eat your supper and sleep well."

Mother secured Tan on her hip and, after pausing briefly, held out a hand for Yuki.

Trying and failing to hide her delight, Yuki eagerly grasped it and danced out of the room. Her plan was coming together. Mother would love her again, if she was myr enough, and then she would kill the shark and Kei and Father would love her again too. Tomorrow, she would prove she wasn't broken.

Tomorrow, she would taste the ocean.

11

Breathe above, breathe below,
take the form of need.
Walk above, swim below,
balance must you heed.
Mindful form, needful form,
the myr must always be.

The Way of the Current

Master Merridan guided Yuki to the Garrison Gate on the edge of the underwater town, near to people but not so busy as the Lower Market. Mother expressly forbade him from leading her to Wen's gate, and he had apparently assumed she didn't want to go the Whale Gate. He was right.

"This is the gate you'll use most often anyhow," he said, guiding her toward the massive portal. The gate was perfectly still, a vertical looking-glass with an entire world beyond.

The garrison sat downslope, its impressive training hall standing out with its domed roof. The barracks adjacent covered a large portion of the sloping shelf, two stories of on-duty soldiers and soldiers-in-training. The various training yards covered every surface outward from the hall, and from here she could see figures sparring in a fluid dance of fins and jianswords. The kelp forest and any coral had been cleared and the ocean floor bricked, and any sand swept away. Here was the heart of Shiggon-jin might.

"Master Sashiro wants me to study there," she mumbled, pointing down the road at the distant hall.

Merridan stroked her hair. "And so you shall, my child. You will become so familiar with this gate and this road, these hard days will be forgotten."

She gazed out with a small, hopeful smile tugging at her cheeks.

Mother had come too, with Tan hoisted on her hip and Kei trailing behind. Although Kei seemed scornfully doubtful, Mother didn't seem as aloof. She had attended the last few lessons regardless of

Tan's presence, checking in regularly and encouraging Yuki as she progressed. She had held Yuki's hand from the castle proper all the way through the mainway. Her slender fingers were strong and comforting, warm in the palm and cool where the metal of her rings sat. She squeezed Yuki's hand lightly before handing her off to Merridan, then settled into a plush chair that had been placed near the gate for her. Tan bounced on her lap, giggling and pulling at the gauzy silk cape hanging from her elbows.

Yuki redirected her attention to Master Merridan. The Waterpriest traversed the portal, shifting himself fully, then turned to assist her. His tail, like the rest of him, was big and round, with an incredible orange-brown streaking over darker scales. His fins matched the burnished flecks in his eyes, with a lighter yellow edging. He clicked instructions, repeating his various mantras just as he had for weeks. He reached through the portal, taking her hand in his, and clicked encouragement.

Flashes of Tai and Wen flickered across her vision, and she almost hiccupped as her breath caught in her throat. The memories struck her in the gut despite how pleasant they were: Tai cupping her small hand in his and keeping her balanced, the brightness of his grin as he dragged her to visit the whales, Wen curling the tactile ends of his arms around her wrist like fingers. With the sights came sounds and smells: the low groan of the sawtooth reverberating through the ocean, followed by Tai's reply, the excited chatter of whale calves as they met new friends, the strongly fishy smell mixed with spices from whatever meal Wen had just eaten.

"You can do this, Yuki-sho." Merridan's voice broke through.

She had frozen in place and realized she was staring through him, her jaw hanging slack and her body tugging backward in resistance. She huffed and battled to slow her pulse, but it pattered in her ears like a galloping horse.

Merridan clicked encouragement again, then drew her gradually toward the gate. He pointed one at a time to his nose, ears, gills, and legs.

She complied.

The moment her nose touched the portal, it shuttered. She blinked, and when she opened her eyes again they had changed, and the water no longer burned. Merridan held her gaze and her hand—*just like Tai would*—and she knew she was safe to focus on the shift. Her ears adjusted to the pressure with a shrill creaking inside, a little pain on the eardrums, and then the rattle of weapons rang clearly from the garrison. The sounds of industry and conversation traveled from the town, and the continuous rustling and popping of the Mana Loi hit her like a wave.

When her gills rippled open, the intoxicating flavor of sweet coral hit her; the tang of kelp and the mineral saltiness of the ocean flowed into her. Father Mana Loi joined with her, filling her with strength and peace. The garrison left a sharp, metallic residue in the water from weaponry and armor; the town left remnants of food from the noon meal. Yuki reached up to touch her gills, verifying that the moment was real.

She shifted her legs last, still leaning on Merridan for balance. She watched as her toes fused, her feet compressed and spread into a tail fin, and her legs melded together. Joy swelled into imperceptible tears, and she trilled her happiness to Master Merridan.

He beamed at her, his own eyes seeming a little red.

Then she glanced back at Mother and Kei.

Mother was no longer in her chair. She stood so close to the gate her nose touched, and she wore a satisfied, prim look. She nodded approval, and relief and warmth flushed through Yuki, easing her limbs and finally calming the pounding in her chest. Tan stood on wobbly legs next to Mother, clapping and smiling, but Kei glowered, her arms crossed and her chin jutting out. Yuki's happiness faded for a moment, but then she decided it didn't matter.

She was home. Finally *home*, one with the water and one with the waves. She could swim, far and long, dancing in the currents and remembering Tai-fun.

For once, her insides didn't turn over at the thought. Tai was her inspiration, her rock, and this was the closest she would ever be to him. In the water, right where she was meant to be. Yuki clicked her excitement again. The sound reminded her of the whales, and she repeated it in a cadence similar to what the sawtooths used to communicate. Merridan smiled.

Mother waved them toward the garrison and returned to her chair to watch. Kei followed her, arms still crossed and shoulders tight. Tan watched longer, collapsing from his wobbly stance to the ground in front of the gate. When she turned away, he was grabbing fistfuls of sand and throwing them with a mischievous laugh.

She could *swim*.

She could swim until she found Wen. She could swim until she found the beast. She could swim until she found a place that reminded her of Taifun, and then she could stay there.

"Shall we visit the arch commodore at the hall?" Master Merridan asked. Even clicking, his voice conveyed a pride she hadn't heard directed at her in so long, it ached.

Yuki nodded, and he led her toward the garrison. They swam hand in hand, enjoying the peaceful trek downslope. The road was wide enough to accommodate a platoon six wide, allowing them to move easily between the garrison and the air-filled mainway, and was kept clear. Along the edges, the life of the ocean sprang up: small coral structures joined by rock to form a border fence of sorts, kelp and other underwater plants, and countless feelers poking from beneath rock ledges.

They were halfway there when a chorus of warnings reverberated through the water from the town. Yuki whipped toward the origin of the cries, her heart clenching in her chest, and scanned the ocean.

A figure swam madly toward them, clicking between breaths to watch out, *watch out!* It was Nurse.

And that was when Yuki saw it.

The beast.

It slid coolly through the streets of the town, visible between buildings, then turned down a main road toward the garrison. It quickened at the sight of the lone, struggling old woman and headed directly toward them.

Yuki felt herself being dragged back toward the gate, but she resisted, unable to take her eyes off the scene. She had to get to Nurse. She had to stop the monstrous blueback, before it was too late.

Merridan wouldn't let go, his grip on her wrist tightening as he chirped commands to return. She pulled, and he pulled back. She sank her teeth into his hand.

He cried out, a ululating trill of pain that carried through the current, and then he released her.

She darted for the floundering figure of her beloved caretaker with his cries following her. Nurse was too old to take on a monster like the one on her tail. Yuki had to save her. She reached Nurse right before the shark did, and it veered from a direct path to a smooth loop around the pair. It evaluated them with black eyes, dispassionate as it cinched tighter and tighter around them.

Nurse wrapped her arms around Yuki. Terror shone in the muddy flecks of her cataract-grayed eyes. "Why did you come, Yuki-sho?" she lamented. "I was trying to warn you."

Yuki didn't answer, intent as she was upon the beast. How could she stop it? The beast was massive, and so powerful. Its scarred side undulated with muscle with each sweep of its tail, and its razored mouth hung open, ready to tear into them at any moment. It was all of her nightmares made real. Horrid images flashed before her as she recalled Tai's last moments. This *was* the monster, the very same one. She blinked the images away. Focus.

She couldn't save Nurse in this form.

Perhaps she could become more.

Yuki locked eyes with the beast, memorizing its fearsome mouth, rough skin, and inverted tail. And she changed. Her body twisted, bones almost snapping they shifted so quickly into unfamiliar shapes. Her innards compressed uncomfortably as the alteration flowed through her body. She abandoned her lungs, and her rib cage folded and crushed into itself. Her head and arms melded into her body, and a searing pain burst through her skull as the change was completed.

Nurse chirped a sharp alarm and released her.

Yuki whipped her head from side to side. It was difficult to think. A deluge of powerful scents hit her. The smells of the town were stronger: the remnants of waterdog waste, human filth and garbage, and the inherently unique odors of individual people. The garrison reeked of metal and blood and leather, of food in the mess hall. The kelp forest smelled of new fruits and fish and greenness.

The beast retreated, still circling with intense hunger but further out than before.

This form wasn't enough to turn it away. Yuki had to be bigger, stronger. In the muddle of her mind, she scanned the sea floor, seeing only sand, rock, and kelp. No one—not Master Merridan and not Sashiro and not Mother—had ever told her this was possible. Nevertheless, she reached out with her fuzzy mind, trying to somehow shift it into her body.

So hard to focus.

The rock dissolved, and its fragments came to bind upon her body, melting seamlessly into skin. The kelp followed. Sand alighted from the ocean floor and streamed onto her fins and form, enveloping her in a dusty, swirling cloud and then becoming part of her.

Her body swelled, becoming as massive as her imagination allowed. Her jaws lengthened, and razor teeth pushed out in endless rows. Her muscles thickened into knotted cords of power and strength. She was ready to confront the monster now; they were the same.

A scream swelled into her mind like the rush of a tidal wave, then ebbed out like a dream, or maybe a nightmare. Nurse's mouth hung slack. Something about it made Yuki angry, like she wanted to snap at the weak, wailing thing. Yuki whipped her head again.

So hard to focus.

The monster, Yuki. It was almost like Tai speaking to her in the fog. His voice sliced through with sharp clarity, and she would have blinked if she had eyelids. This form was so strange, so unfamiliar, and yet it enveloped her more thoroughly than any disguise. This was *her*, entirely her, melded with Father Mana Loi and one with the Water.

The shark had retreated, slowing its predatory circling to stare coldly at this new threat. Then it attacked, siphoning through the ocean toward Nurse with its jaws wide.

Yuki burst forward and snapped at it, grazing its pectoral fin and tearing a series of lines open along its side. The shark turned away from Nurse and headed back out, glaring with hate.

The taste of blood excited her; it filtered through her teeth and into her throat. If she'd had a tongue, she would have licked her lips. She wanted more.

But the beast stayed back, seeming to reevaluate its options as it bled freely into the ocean. Yuki held her ground, challenging it directly with her body language and black gaze. This was it. Either it would die, or she would, and if she did die, she would join the current with her brother. At least Nurse would have a chance to live.

The beast charged again, but then a harpoon pierced its side with a thump. The creature writhed as more blood exploded from the wound. Yuki could *taste* it, and it was glorious. The tether tightened and held. Several more harpoons hit the creature, and it twisted back and forth in pain.

In Yuki's cloudy mind, she realized the garrison had arrived. Soldiers appeared everywhere, shooting bolts into the beast's side and pulling it with tethers to the ocean floor. Harpoons jabbed through every fin, yanking the beast taut in every direction, and then a single soldier approached and shoved a large blade through its skull.

The monster, *her* monster, spasmed with one last violent twitch, then stilled.

Yuki saw everything happen as though in a dream. The harpoons flew in slow motion, and their strike into rough skin thundered like the booming of a great drum. Blood poured from the creature's wounds in a gentle plume of crimson, a burst of delectable death that flooded Yuki's senses. The chaos of sounds—the clink of weapons against hips, the scrape of body movement, the rasp of scale mail—engulfed her.

She watched intently as the shadowy malignance of the beast's gaze dulled to nothing.

And that was its end.

The monster was gone. If it had a soul, she hoped it passed to a lower gate, but she didn't think she believed such a horrible thing could have a soul. Was it better for it to just be dead, nonexistent, or for it to suffer for tearing everything she loved apart? She didn't know, but as its last spasms stopped, she realized she didn't feel much better.

In the muddle of her reflections, she noted the soldiers shifting their attention. They clicked at each other in words she should have recognized, then approached cautiously. She dimly recognized the reloading of bolts and harpoons, and she moved to block them from Nurse. The elderly woman had stopped screaming, which was good because the sound had hurt Yuki's ability to think.

Yuki didn't understand this shift in events, but she felt fear creeping through the length of her massive body, tingling through her fins and telling her to lash out before it was too late. Nerves fired, and everything in her tensed, prepared to spring forward and gnash at the first body she reached. The bloody flavor of the ocean made her hungry for more, and the aggressive things approaching her with pointed weapons could provide it to her.

But Nurse appeared in front of her, one hand toward Yuki and one toward the soldiers. She clicked reassurances. All is well. All is well. It's the princess. All is well. The soldiers checked, glancing warily at each other with spearguns shouldered. The harpooners held their weapons at the ready, trained upon Yuki, and their fingers shook over the triggers.

An officer appeared at the edge of Yuki's vision, commanding they stand down. Was that Uncle Sash? Why was it so hard to recognize anyone? She whipped her head again, trying to break through the haze, and the soldiers flinched as one. The officer waved his hands, a motion that excited her for some reason, but then the soldiers began to back away.

"It's all right now, Yuki-sho." Nurse spoke directly to her, her arm still outstretched. Her hand trembled as she reached out to caress Yuki's cheek.

Yuki resisted the impulse to snap at her.

"It's all right, dearie," Nurse continued. Her wrinkled hand stroked from Yuki's snout toward her gills. "Can you shift back?"

She stared stupidly for moments, letting the words wash over her. They bounced through her head without meaning at first, then coalesced. Shift back. She focused, as Master Merridan trained her to do. It hurt in her skull. Her ears screamed and her temples flared with a strange fire of confusion.

But once she had shifted her head, her thoughts became clearer. She could better concentrate on altering her chest and shoulders, her lungs and spine. Her fins projected out and lengthened to scrawny arms once again. Sandy dust wafted off her as she shed excess mass, finally emerging from the cloud as a slight-bodied myr girl.

She drifted, rubbing her eyes and shaking her arms out. Her body felt utterly confused, and her re-formed tongue didn't seem to know how to react to the richness of blood in the water.

Nurse gawked but never let go of her cheek. Now she tapped Yuki's nose with a forefinger and attempted a smile. "I knew you were in there, dearie. Thank you for saving me." Then, despite the shaking in the old woman's limbs, she pulled Yuki into a protective hug.

Waterpriest Merridan appeared. He alternated between staring at Yuki with awe and staring shame-faced at the sea floor. Had he hidden? He removed his own longshirt and pulled it over Yuki's head, and she realized her clothes had ripped apart during her final shift. Her tunic, her breechbelt, all of it was gone.

Master Sashiro's clicking shouts reached her, and she saw the soldiers disperse. Most returned to the garrison while a few cleaned up the carcass of the massive monster. Then the arch commodore approached them. He examined her for a long time, saying nothing, until she suddenly realized she hadn't greeted him properly.

She saluted with both hands and looked at his chest. "Sir."

Sashiro opened his mouth as though to speak, but nothing came out. Then he swam forward and adjusted her oversized longshirt, straightening it to cover her better. He seemed to check all of her limbs for injuries, his face stiffened to avoid expression.

"I'm okay, sir," she mumbled.

Master Sashiro tipped her chin up and peered into her face. "Yes, I believe you are," he answered. Then he glanced up to her head, and the way he ran his big hand over her skull made her realize she must have lost her hair. How funny she must look! Sashiro inspected her head and face once more, then released her. "You will be a strong Second, Taiuki. You *are* a strong Second." The slightest hint of astonishment revealed his feelings, and Yuki felt a small bit of pride well up.

She had impressed him. She had done something difficult, something impossible, and she had saved Nurse. She hadn't really gotten to kill the beast like she wanted, but it *was* dead. It was a small comfort, although less fulfilling than she had expected.

He dismissed her with a formal gesture, then turned back to oversee the carcass cleanup.

Nurse and Master Merridan both took her hands and guided her back to the Garrison Gate. Mother and Kei both stood beyond the portal, their jaws dropped. Kei's round eyes looked like they might fall out of her head. Tan patted the surface of the Gate and howled with happy giggles, which escalated further when he saw her getting closer.

They stepped through the gate, shifting to human form as a group. Yuki still felt strange, muddled, and she leaned on both helping hands as her legs emerged from the tail. Then she broke into a satisfied smile.

Tan ambled over to them first, babbling with delight and pointing through the gate, then grasping Yuki's legs. He had learned with her, achieved the shift to myrform at her side—although his little fin was chubby with that roly-poly roundness that she always wanted to squeeze—and now he'd seen her take a leap forward into something else. He grinned up at her, clutching the edge of her tunic.

He screeched when Mother seized him. Her expression was stone, and she backed away from Yuki at a measured, carefully elegant pace. She swallowed several times, blinking repeatedly.

"Mama? Did you see me?"

Mother opened her mouth, parting her beautifully ochred lips to speak, then closed it again.

"She saved me, Your Highness," Nurse ventured in a quivering voice. Her gaze was on the floor in deference to the queen.

Mother's bewilderment shifted to irritation. "Don't speak to me. You have no place here." She shifted a squirming Tan to her other hip, then directed her attention to Yuki. "How did . . ." She didn't finish, seeming entirely unsure of what to say. Yuki had never seen Mother lack for eloquence, but she seemed lost in this moment.

Master Merridan interjected politely. "A godly form, Your Highness. One with the Most High . . . No one has achieved such a shift in a long time. Truly one with the Water, and the Water is one with her." He beamed at Yuki.

But Mother wrinkled her nose and backed up another step, her face laden with doubt. "I must tell Rentai." She turned and hurried away. Tan screamed, flailing his arms and legs out and finally clambering high enough to look over Mother's shoulder. He reached a pudgy hand out to Yuki as Mother receded down the mainway.

Kei still stood behind the spot Mother had vacated, frozen with fright. They joined looks for only a moment before she gasped and ran after Mother, her skirt and cape fluttering behind her. She didn't look back, and her footsteps faded to a distant patter.

In the subsequent silence surrounding the Garrison Gate, Yuki's heart fell, and a new sorrow settled upon her scrawny shoulders.

This was a different feeling. Not like Tai's death, a tragic thing she couldn't stop. Not like being cut off from the ocean by her own mind and body, which she could overcome. This was something else, a conscious rejection of who she was by those who were closest to her. She couldn't change that.

She looked to Master Merridan, and he tightened his hold of her hand. "Be at ease, my little Yuki-sho. They may not appreciate it yet, but you have more of the ocean in you than most. You may be different, but not because you are broken. Your myr blood is stronger than any I've ever known, and someday they'll see that too."

Nurse echoed the Waterpriest's words.

Yuki tried to understand, but all she could see was that the hallway was empty. Empty save for the remnant flavors of blood and fear that hung in the air, both palpable to her heightened senses.

Empty.

12

"Do you see it, Kei? There, it's her. Come look." Yuki pulled at her older sister's hand, but Kei leaned the opposite way and remained on the couch, her feet tucked up on the cushions with a light fur on top.

"I don't care," came Kei's bored tone from behind her book.

Yuki rushed along the massive picture window and pushed her nose against the cold glass. She strained to see through the gray murkiness toward the migratory route followed by the wild sawtooths, but all she could see were vague shapes. One had come close enough that she was sure that was what they were. It was the pod that always passed close to Shiggo City, the one with the friendly cow.

Yuki looked back at Kei. "Will you come with me?"

"No."

Yuki pouted her lip out, then wrenched a smaller side window open.

"Mama doesn't like when you go through windows," Kei muttered from behind her book.

"Mama doesn't like anything I do," Yuki retorted, squeezing through the narrow portal.

"True enough." At first, that seemed like all Kei was going to say, but then she slammed her book shut with an exasperated huff. "But maybe she wouldn't be so annoyed if you didn't do things like that. Why can't you just conform to her rules? Why can't you just be normal?"

Yuki didn't answer, instead sticking her tongue out. She squeezed her slim frame through the picture window. She'd swim to the pod alone.

"You're bringing the consequences on yourself," said Kei, reopening her book and flipping her hair.

Yuki ignored her.

The blue silhouette, at first far off, drifted south and westward, skirting the edge of Shiggo City and following the chute that rushed down from the straits.

Yuki attempted to call to it, mimicking the rumbling groan they made, the one she had heard Tai make. Her voice couldn't go that low, even with the changes in her throat from the shift, but a sound of sorts came out. She tried again, this time better but still awkward.

The gray-blue shape turned toward her, sluggish in its reactions, and she hastened toward it.

She chirped happy greetings to it, even as her own memories tore at her dragging fins. How good it was to see her, after her long journey north! How beautiful she was! How long her journey must have been!

The dowager clicked a reply, but something was wrong. She didn't dart up and down, and her tan splotches were a dulled beige. Her browns were the color of dead winter grass, and her eyes lacked the spark of life they had once held. She was missing a pectoral fin, and a terrible gash ran along her side. The wound wasn't fresh, but it wasn't old either. The skin still looked tender, red and pink streaks cutting across the white and grayish brown of her side.

Yuki clicked in dismay, which escalated to gut-wrenching apprehension. "What happened to your baby?" She peered beyond the matron whale, toward the rest of the pod. She recognized the cow's offspring from years prior, but there was no tiny calf hiding behind her tail, shy and soft and innocent.

The whale responded with a high wail, one that carried to the rest of the pod, which turned to wait for her. She whipped her head and tail, as though trying to reject the cruel reality. They wailed back.

The calf was dead.

Yuki clicked reassurances and stroked the whale's nose, then trailed her hand back along its side. She didn't touch the injuries, but she could tell they were wicked gashes and tears. Teeth. A shark had gotten her—and her baby too.

She sobbed, then projected all her empathy and mourning to the whale. She returned to the whale's head and looked her in the eye. "I'm so sorry. I lost my brother. Do you remember him?"

The whale repeated her moan, a creaking sound so full of anguish that Yuki thought, animal or not, she really did understand.

"He joined the current a few weeks after you passed through in the spring," Yuki murmured, rambling. She knew the whale's vocabulary wasn't this advanced, but they were bonded by loss regardless of their ability to formulate their tragedies into words. She stroked the whale's mottled nose and continued. "He was so excited to meet your littlest one. Maybe they'll take care of each other in the next Gate, at least until we can see them again."

The whale groaned a plaintive response.

Yuki held back another shudder. The ocean could hide her tears, but not her quavering breath. But officers shouldn't cry, so she wouldn't. Hardening herself, she thought back to those precious moments: Tai's grin, higher on the left than the right, the opposite direction from the way he could quirk his eyebrows. His hand on hers, guiding her, balancing her, giving her a foundation upon which she could pour her trust. That spring was both yesterday and an eternity in the past.

"Tai also said not to be sad because life must move forward," she clicked softly, wishing with all her heart that the whale could respond and help her understand that herself. "I don't see how life can move forward without him, though. I'm not supposed to be Second, and now I'm training with the arch commodore every day, plus these strange magika lessons that seem to frighten half of the people around me. Keiki is training to be queen, and she's not even nice. How can you be queen of an entire kingdom of people if you're not nice?"

The cow nickered at her, a surprisingly domestic sound for a wild whale.

"You would know. You're a leader in your pod, and you're one of the nicest whales I've ever met." Yuki attempted a smile, but it was really just a stretching of her cheeks into a wistful expression of uncertainty. "I just don't see how life can move forward, but it does, I guess."

The great dowager blinked at her, seeming to take all her words in the way that Wen used to do, then released an ear-piercing keen and moved away. She circled once and invited Yuki to join her as the pod moved south.

"Go with the current," Yuki chirped after her, raising an arm in farewell.

The whale first became a blurry shape, then melted into the deep blue ocean with her family. From Shiggo, they would move southwest to the Lai'akala Trench, then cut southward along its edge to Riyogo, and then to the warm, pleasant waters of Tedami.

Yuki watched until she was certain they were gone, then turned back toward the castle. Without the whale's presence, she was a lone speck in the Mana Loi, out swimming alone. Something Mother said she should never do. She hurried back to the window she had left open, but when she got there, the window had been closed and latched.

Princess Taiuki, Second of Shiggo, will return in The Keepers of Midgate

Afterword

WANT MORE OF MIDGATE?

Myrmaiden is set in the world of Midgate, where elemental magic flows through people and elusive dragons lurk in the abandoned corners. Myrpeople carry Water magika in their blood, a boon and a curse as they are rejected by humans, and vice versa. Other races carry the magika of Earth, Fire, Air, and Sun, yielding a diversity of peoples and cultures.

Set after *Myrmaiden*, the epic fantasy *The Keepers of Midgate* follows multiple characters in disparate parts of the world, including Taiuki, the fearless Second of Shiggo. Each character seeks to right the wrongs they face, to break free of the bonds of society. As they forge onward, they are drawn toward a greater calling, to face and defeat the madness that is tearing their world apart. Check out the first book, *Liberation*, at:

https://rmkrogman.com/books/liberation/

Read More by R. M. Krogman

Keepers of Midgate

Recommended Reading Order
Liberation
Myrmaiden: A Story of Midgate
Sundering
Schism

Additional Stories of Midgate
Marked (Novella)
Desert Rose (Novella)
The Chronicles of Thordrin (Novella)

About the Author

REBECCA M. KROGMAN IS an epic and dark fantasy author from Iowa, USA.

Her debut novel, *Liberation*, is the first volume of a larger story set in Midgate, a medieval-inspired world of magic, mermaids, and wyverns. She has been developing the *Keepers of Midgate* epic since she was in high school. The main storyline has changed little since then, only gaining more clarity and detail as the characters take on a life of their own. The world has grown in its depth of history, culture, and geography, spawning numerous side stories, prequels, and a sequel.

She loves nature, art, and food, which all funnel into her world-building. Her story's settings span two continents and the sea between, encompassing a diversity of peoples, cultures, and creatures. She is working on a collection of recipes from Midgate, and she loves drawing scenes and characters from the books (although those sketches may never see the light of day). She will never apologize for describing a tree, as she finds trees to be fascinating and far more alive than they get credit for.

When she's not writing about Midgate, she's penning fairy tale retellings. She enjoys mixing familiar pieces from many tales together and may one day reveal to you her *Tinderbox Princess* series.